CAUGHT IN THE SLUICE

Tales from Alaska's Gold Camps

Neil Davis

McRoy and Blackburn
Publishers

Table of Contents

Moose John, A Miner's Tale

Long before Moose John came to Ester City, the miners in the camps scattered all the way from Dawson downriver to Rampart knew of him. They were used to meeting him along the trails or seeing him walk past their diggings, and they talked about him because he was the only man they knew who could carry an entire moose.

That was a sort of miner's tale—the kind that a miner upon hearing had to pretend neither to disbelieve nor believe. If he indicated disbelief, it was likely to rile the teller, even if the words sounded preposterous. Worse yet, the doubting listener might later find himself the fool. But on the other hand, if the listener appeared to accept the questionable story at face value, he would seem naive. The only thing to do was make a noncommittal remark, maybe something like, "Yup, that's a lot of meat for one man to carry," with just the right tone that could be construed to convey either acceptance or skepti-

cism. Perhaps then the teller would make further remark to indicate the degree of truth. That might
take some minutes or even several days, if both teller
and listener were skilled at verbal parrying.

The miners' code said that a man should work
hard and talk little. Thus, a given conversation might
stretch on for weeks, being dropped as two men
parted and then resumed again on their next meeting. If they were partners working together, they
might have ten conversations going at once. It was a
test of a man's mental ability to pick up on a remark
that referred to something said three days before,
but the conversational pace did allow a man to mull
over what to say next.

Moose John's ability to carry a moose made for a
good-telling story because it was both true and false.
He was big, and obviously strong, but it was beyond
belief that any man could carry a thousand-pound
moose out of the woods. But if one scoffed he soon
learned that Moose John did indeed carry out a
whole moose, even if he left behind the head, the
hide, all the bones and the poorest of the meat.
When John finished butchering, he was left with
limpish masses of dark-red flesh, collectively weighing two hundred to three hundred pounds. That was
still more than most men would want to carry, but
John was big, and he knew how to do it.

Moose John piled the meat onto squares of canvas, tied them into tight bundles, two or three of
them, and then lashed them to his outsize
packboard. With the big pack standing upright on

the ground, or perhaps elevated slightly on a log, he sat before it and pulled the straps onto his shoulders. Moose John then rolled over onto his hands and knees with the load on his back. He tied the pack's waistband around his belly and fixed its tumpline to his forehead. The hardest part was standing up. Holding two walking sticks in his hands, John would rise on his knees and then pull himself up, muscled cords flaring out from his neck as they took up the strain transmitted down from John's head.

Once he was upright, John's next secret was to walk slowly, put weight on the walking sticks held in each hand—and never stop. Moose John himself weighed just over two hundred pounds and was slightly over six feet tall. Big, but not truly huge, John had wide shoulders and a spare frame so tightly muscled that he looked almost gaunt. Fully loaded, he was an awesome spectacle to anyone meeting him on the trail. Four or five hundred pounds of Moose John and moose meat methodically moved along as John's arms reached forward from wide shoulders, alternately pushing and pulling on the walking sticks, much like drive rods on a locomotive. John's unhurried gait might seem very slow to anyone who met him out in the wilderness, but it persisted uphill and downhill, and it put the miles behind. When John ambled into a miner's camp to sell his meat, the visit was good for a week of discussion there.

"Migawd, George, that was a heavy pack Moose was carrying."

(The next day.) "Did you see Shorty try to lift that pack? Couldn't even get it off the ground."

(A day or two later.) "Funny thing, you ever see that big Swede rest, except in camp? Never heard of anyone who ever saw Moose John in the woods when he wasn't moving. I hear tell that ol' Moose never even sits down once he's loaded."

(Several days later.) "Edgar Olsen over on Hopeless Creek saw Moose John go past one day last fall carrying three caribou. Sure as hell wouldn't catch me out there carrying all that meat as far as Moose John does, and then selling it for fifteen cents a pound."

John, on the other hand, walked away from a miners' camp thinking about how he sure wouldn't work hard like the miners did, grubbing all day in the dirt or getting cold hands from panning in the frigid waters. Hunting was a better way to live, he thought. Didn't pay much, but then a man like him didn't need much. Just enough money for shells, a few groceries and once in a while a new pair of boots or pants. John knew he usually could find an old cabin to stay in near most of the diggings, or if not, he could build one in a few days. He spent much of the time out on the trail anyway, camping wherever he found himself when tired or it was too dark to move on.

Aside from knowing how to cut up game and lighten it, and how to get a heavy pack up off the ground, John's main secret to carrying his monstrous loads was the thinking. He'd learned early that if he thought about other things as he walked along, he could forget the bands cutting into his shoulders and across his forehead, and be unconscious of the ache in his back and legs. He could walk for miles that way, giving no more thought to perambulating than to breathing, just letting his legs and fringes of his mind direct him along through the woods or on a trail. A mile or two could disappear that way, with John being in no more agony or little more tired than at its start. He could easily go forty miles in a day with a light pack, and carrying a full load for ten, maybe fifteen, if the going wasn't too rough. Just let the eyes defocus and move slowly along, thinking, just thinking; thinking about anything.

John could think about events in the past or dream of things to come; it mattered little. Regardless of how many times he had relived a past event, he could live it again, repeating exactly as before, or thinking about it in a new way. He could start at the beginning of a happening, at the end, or anywhere in between; it mattered not, nor did it matter if events got mixed up together. While John plodded a hundred yards down a trail under a heavy load, his mind could soar through time and space, to places and events experienced or those not, dwelling there until his thoughts turned elsewhere, or perhaps until the movement of an animal or the new vista revealed by the turning of the trail pulled his brain back to help lean against the tumpline.

'Thar she blows, Captain John, off to starboard.'...'Bring her two points over, Steersman.' (This was a favorite, an oft-repeated boyhood dream.) 'Lower the longboat; I'll take the harpoon

on this one.'...'Good thrust, Captain, you got him.'
Foot up on the bobbing bow, Captain John could
see the blood spreading across the water and hear
the rope whistling out past his leg....'Bring her about;
heave boys, run with him...run....Run, John-John,
run, don't let them catch us. There's no worse gang
in town than that bunch of toughs'...He fell, but
when they caught up he was fighting, flailing out
wildly at the air and then connecting with a face. The
big boy staggered back, and soon they were gone.
'You sure hit him hard, John-John; bet they don't
mess around with us never again...never
again...Never again, we'll never see Papa again,' His
mother was sobbing, and as they walked away with
her arm across his shoulders, John looked back to
see the man shoveling the dirt over his father's coffin. 'Oscar, you're the man of the family now. You'll
have to help me take care of Hilda, Anna and little
John-John....John Johansen, Oscar Johansen, Albert
Dall, Charley Larsen, Wilber Kuggen...' the man
with the clipboard and the thick handlebar mus-
tache called out the names of the boarding passengers. John walked up the gangway behind Oscar
onto the little steamer taking them north to Skagway
and the Klondike gold fields beyond. Strange feeling, that, walking onto a ship for the first time, sens-
ing the vibrations of the engine through the soles of
his feet. Then, as darkness fell, they were pulling out
from Seattle, seeing the lights of the town reflected
in the widening black water...'Water, give me water,'
old Alex gasped, his last dying words, as he lay back
against the pillow, clutching one hand across his

chest...Clutching one hand across her breast, Mary Ellen gasped, 'Oh, you frightened me. I didn't know anyone was about.' She was so beautiful sitting there on the moss with her long dark hair spread across her back and with one tuft curled forward over her shoulder, almost to her waist...And so it went, mile after mile of trail falling behind him, lost amidst the wandering thoughts.

As long as he could remember, John could submerge pain or unwanted feeling in thoughts, and he developed the ability more fully as the years went by. Just the thinking about something else carried him through the tough hungry times back in New York after Papa died. The thinking made bearable the uncomfortable hours spent in the smelly hold of that little coastal steamer as it slowly churned up through the Inside Passage, and it lessened the miseries of that first far northern winter on the Klondike and any number of other uncomfortable times. During the years that followed, John's thinking and dreaming also kept him from being lonely when he sat in a cabin on the fringes of one of the mining camps, waiting for better hunting weather.

John always had an ample supply of chewed-over thoughts to turn to, but when his association with Mary Ellen developed, whole new worlds opened up. Before meeting her, John's thought repertoire had a limited emotional range. Depending upon what he chose to think about, he could conjure up feelings of contentment or pangs of sorrow. After Mary Ellen came into his life, John's thought sym-

phonies encompassed new ranges of ideas and emotions. Thoughts about Mary Ellen's great beauty or
the trilling of her laughter gave John prolonged peri-
ods of happiness and a gnawing hope for the future
that he had never felt previously. Thinking of her, he
could soar into ecstasy, to a level of rapture never before achieved, or he could plunge himself into a
gloomy depression. Before Mary Ellen, thoughts
about Papa, Oscar's untimely death or other somber
matters merely saddened John. Afterwards, such
heavy-hearted remembrances brought a grief that
caused him to cry silently inside, and, if he was not
careful, to settle into a deep, lasting melancholy.
Mary Ellen made him more alive, but less in control.
Little matter, that; overall, she had brought great
happiness and purpose to John's life.

If meeting Mary Ellen was one part of the pivot
about which John's mental journeys now turned, old
Alex's death was the other. They created the start of
his new life after he came to Ester City.

John hadn't cared much for the town when he arrived there from Rampart, and was almost ready to
move on elsewhere when he met Alex. Poor old
Alex, sitting there outside his cabin above the town,
so weak he could barely walk...'I'm Moose John; got
the little cabin up the hill, over across the
valley'...'Well, hello, Moose John; I'm Alex
Vladovich. I ain't feeling so good today. Guess I'll go
in and rest.'...'Here, I'll give you a hand...there you
go. Cool in here; time for a fire. Say, I got two spruce
hens I just shot. How's about I cook one up for you?

Yeah, I'll do that; you just rest easy a while, Mr. Vladovich'...Putting off his plans to leave Ester...going back to care for Alex each day...the old man getting weaker as time passed, talking little except on that last day...'John, you ain't got much except for your guns and stuff. Me, I got this nice cabin here and this mine. Go get Alfy and Joe down at their place below the hill'...'Hello, Alfy; hello, Joe. Boys, I ain't doing too well lately. I just might not make it. If I don't, I want you fellows to witness that I'm giving my cabin and my claim here to Moose John.'...Alfy and Joe are gone; Alex is lying there, pale, breathing fitfully. He rises up on his elbows to stare at John out of sunken eyes, suddenly bright with excitement. 'John, she's rich. Ain't never told anyone how much gold she carries. You can't see the gold, either. She's all locked up in the quartz, John, got to mill it out. You'll see the vein in the tunnel. Take the good stuff and she runs a hundred dollars a bucket. I'm gonna die, John, so she's yours, the gold and everything. Be real careful, you got to...' Clasping one hand across his chest, Alex fell back on the bed, too weak to go on...'Water, give me water,' and then he was gone....

Late evening, almost midnight, with the sun just down. It's sad digging Alex's grave, but it is a pretty place up there behind the cabin, on the knoll of the hill...The sun comes up and the birds begin their morning songs again, just as John piles up the last of the rocks around the wooden cross on Alex's covered resting place...Poor old Alex, but his dying had made John rich, and if he hadn't stayed on in Ester City to care for Alex, John would have been without Mary Ellen, too.

Beautiful Mary Ellen. Without question, John's favorite thinking about her was that day they met, just over a year after Alex died. No day passed that John did not relive that scene, although of late, there was much thinking about what life was going to be like with Mary Ellen when they moved to San Francisco...'John dear, shall we walk down to the shops today?'...'Of course, my dear, it is such a pleasant morning.'...John puts on his hat and stands admiring Mary Ellen's lovely back and the sweep of her dress curving out over her hips and flaring around her unseen feet. She is standing there before the mirror, tying on her bonnet. She smiles at his image in the mirror and winks happily, almost seductively. Arms linked, they stride out the wide door, down the steps lined with flowers. They saunter through the cast-iron gate and are on the walk, ambling casually down the street. Mary Ellen's skirt brushes softly against his trouser leg with each step....

'Good morning, Mrs. Anderson. Nice day, isn't it?'

'That it is, and a good morning to you, Mrs. Johansen. My, you look charming. A lovely new dress you are wearing.'

'Thank you, Mrs. Anderson. John bought it for me just yesterday. He is so good to me.'...John is in the garage on Powell Street. 'Yes sir, Mr. Johansen, we can have the Dodge ready for you tomorrow. Must give it a final check and polish it up proper. Will you be trading in the roadster?'

'I think not. My wife Mary Ellen does love to ride in it on weekends when we go to our beach cottage. Yes, we will keep it. Handy to have two autocars, you know.'

'Yes sir, Mr. Johansen, always a pleasure to do business with a man like you, a man of means, a man who knows what he wants; a real pleasure, sir.'

Such events—those yet to happen—gave John ample latitude for different approaches to them...'Oh John, look at that dress. Isn't it lovely?'

'It certainly is, my dear, let's go in so you can have it fitted.'

'But it looks so expensive!'

'Tut, tut; you forget that we are rich. We will go in and I will buy it for you.'

'Oh, John, you are so good to me. You buy me everything I ever want. I am so happy to be your wife; you are the finest man I have ever known. Shall we sail to Europe again this year?'

'I believe we will go to the Orient, instead. We can sail right here from San Francisco, instead of taking that long train ride to New York. It will be much easier, and you can take all your clothes along. Perhaps we will even take the maid with us to help take care of them and to help you dress.'

'Sounds wonderful, John; we will have much fun, won't we?'

'Of course, my dear, now you run along home. I must stop down to the garage and order that touring car. A Dodge, this time. Yes, I'll buy one of those; fine machine, they say, one of the best, and to us, the cost does not matter.'

By golly, having a beautiful woman for a wife and being rich was mighty fine; gave a man all sorts of things to think about. Of course John was not yet married to Mary Ellen, but there was no question about her acceptance of his proposal. She liked him a lot, and she didn't even know how much gold he had. He'd thought about telling her right at the start. Had almost blurted it out to her that first day, just to make sure she would see him again, but now he was glad he hadn't. Would he have ever known that she loved him for himself, not just because he was rich? As time wore on, he had decided to do it all at once. It was almost time now, just a few weeks more to be spent in old Alex's mine before John would have at least a hundred thousand dollars' worth of gold. That would last Mary Ellen and him all their lives together. John had rehearsed the proposal and the telling about his fortune many times. Sometimes he went through it so that he would get her acceptance before telling her about the gold, and during other rehearsals he reversed the order. Lately, he had pretty much decided to tell her about the gold first, or at least to let her know he was a man of means before asking her to marry him. Yes, that was the way to do it. Boy, was she going to be surprised, and so was everybody else in Ester City—not one of them knew what he had.

However, John admitted to himself, it would have been fun this last year to have shared his secret with

Mary Ellen, to have spent evenings with her talking and dreaming about their future together.

'Oh, John, you've been working so hard for us down in that cold old mine. You must be very tired tonight'....'Not at all, my dear. I'm strong. Never get tired, especially when I think of you, of coming here for tea in the evening after a good day's work. Took out a lot of ore today, better than five hundred dollars' worth. Just think what that will buy. Yes, even before you knew my little secret about the gold, it was fun to sit and have tea with you. You make such good tea, Mary Ellen. I've always enjoyed your tea, and sitting here with you, even before we became such good friends...good friends who will always be together. You know what I mean?'

'Oh yes, John, I do; it will be so much fun, won't it.'...No, that didn't make sense—he hadn't proposed to Mary Ellen; she wouldn't know that he meant to marry her. Oh well, it made no difference really. There was plenty of pleasure in drinking tea and chatting with Mary Ellen even if she didn't know about the gold.

The gold had not come easily, and the early aversion to gold mining that John developed during his one winter at Dawson had not helped. John remembered that winter of 1897-98 well, but he did not like to think much about it.

Oscar and he had gotten to the gold field late that fall. All the good mining ground was already staked, so they went in on a lay on Bonanza Creek with Sam Finley and Peter Gorsen. It was hard work thawing

down through the frozen muck. Twenty feet deep it
was before they got to pay, and the claim's owner got
half of what gold they dug out. Most of the other half
went to Dawson with Oscar, Sam and Peter, while
John stayed in the cabin to tend the fire. Sometimes
they were gone for two days. When they came back,
they often carried more whiskey home than food,
and sometimes they brought no food at all. John disliked both Sam and Peter. They bickered with each
other, and sometimes with Oscar; mostly they ig-
nored John except to chastise him:

'Goddammit, kid, you let the fire go out again. I
ain't never seen anybody who could sit around just
thinking so much he'd forget to put wood in the fire.
Someday your dumb ass is going to freeze to that
stool.' Or, 'Hell, kid, you got to pay more attention
to what you're doing; you slopped every bit of gold
out of that pan. Keep your mind on your job, kid.'

Worse yet, Oscar, especially if he had been drinking, fell in with them and treated John the same way.
One cold night when the food was almost gone, Oscar, Sam and Peter came back from Dawson very
drunk. John could hear them singing and cursing as
they neared the cabin, He was furious when they
staggered in and he saw that they had brought no
food. Usually, the fifteen-mile walk back from
Dawson sobered them up by the time they got
home, but on this trip they had been drinking along
the trail. They still had part of one bottle when they
arrived. After passing it around among the three of
them until it was gone, they crawled into their bunks
and slept.

John could still remember how mad and hungry he had been. Finally, he too had gone to bed, slept fitfully, and awakened early the next morning. The others still snored noisily. The fire was out, and John had begun his normal morning chore of building it when his anger returned. Instead of lighting the fire, he had quickly dressed in his warmest clothes. Then he had taken down the rifle that he and Oscar had bought in Seattle and walked out the door.

The temperature outside had dropped during the night. As John laced on his snowshoes, he felt the frigid air cut against his cheeks, and his breath steamed out in billowing clouds. He could feel the cold seeping through his pants where his bent knee stretched against them. Once the snowshoes were on, John had walked quickly down the trail toward Dawson. The sun would not be up for several hours, but John had no trouble seeing because the full moon shining down on the snow brought an unreal blue-white clarity to the valley of Bonanza Creek.

John walked briskly for several miles. Except for the cold penetrating the cloth around his legs, John was warm, although he frequently had to brush his mitten across his eyes to sweep away the frost that stuck his eyelids together when he blinked.

Then came the happening that gave Moose John his name. John had walked out of the cabin not so much to go hunting as just to get away. He had fired the rifle only a few times before, just when he and Oscar had been practicing with it. The only animal he had ever killed before was a squirrel, one that pranced out on a spruce limb to chatter at them as they were shooting at bottles.

Just before coming to where the trail turned to follow the Klondike River down to Dawson, John saw the moose tracks cutting across his path. He was not sure, but they seemed fresh, perhaps made since the others staggered up from Dawson the night before. John turned off the trail to follow them, at once finding the going difficult in the soft, deep snow. He was sweating and breathing hard after only a few hundred yards. John was fighting his way through a patch of alders, trying to keep the awkward snow-shoes pointed straight ahead, and the snow from falling down his neck as it dumped from disturbed branches, when he heard a deep snort. A great tremor shot through John's body as he saw the moose's head rise up from the snow where the animal was lying, just fifteen or twenty feet in front of him.

As he remembered it, everything transpired in slow motion, although, in fact, it was all over in five seconds. John froze as the moose, a gaunt cow, pushed her head upward on her front feet to stare at him. A cloud of ice particles rose up past her long ears as she exhaled. She was just starting to get her rear legs under her when John flipped off his mitten, cocked the gun, and placed its stock against his thigh, holding the weapon only in his right hand. In the same motion he pulled the trigger. The sound of the gun going off was shockingly loud, and as the muffled echoes rang back from the quiet hillsides nearby, the cow collapsed back onto her snowy bed. The bullet had entered exactly between her eyes, blowing fragments of skull into her brain to destroy instantly all its control over her bony body.

Then John had shaken so uncontrollably that he could barely hold the gun. Several minutes passed before he recovered enough to search for his mitten and get it forced back onto his freezing fingers. When John approached the moose he was staggered by its immense size, and the fact that he had killed it without even aiming the gun properly.

Having shot the moose, John did not know what to do next. Pondering the problem for some minutes, he finally cut one ear from the animal and headed back to the cabin, just as day was dawning. The excitement drained John of the anger he felt toward Oscar, Sam and Peter. They were still abed when he burst into the cold cabin and spewed out a torrent of words to tell them of his deed, swinging the bloody ear before them for proof. Despite their hangovers, the three soon got excited, too. They were hungry—and tired of the primary diet of beans and cornbread they had existed on for weeks.

When the day was done, the moose meat was hung up outside the cabin, except for what they had given to other miners along the creek nearby. John was tired but happy—this was the first time Sam and Peter had treated him almost as an equal. They even laughed and joked with him. That night, as they went to bed after a long meal of fresh meat, it was Peter who said, "Well, Moose, you did well today; I guess we'd all be mighty hungry right now if it weren't for you."

The name Peter gave him stuck. They started

calling him "Moose" regularly, as did others up and down the creek when they heard that John had shot a moose without even aiming his gun. After that, John started going hunting regularly. No one objected when he said he was going out to look for meat when it was time to work down in the shaft. While the others dug, John tramped along the snow-covered hills and valleys. Three weeks went by before John found another moose, up near the head of the valley, far above the camp. This time he aimed. The moose, hit in the side, ran almost half a mile before dying. John gutted and cut the moose up by himself, and dragged it in pieces back to the cabin, using the sled he had built just for the purpose. They now had more meat than they needed, so John sold half of the second moose to some other miners for three ounces of gold. He kept the money, and the others did not object.

It was a happy time for John. He disliked the work in the shaft, and he liked doing something for himself, out away from the others. While John hunted, they dug, and they still spent most of their earnings in Dawson's saloons. One night Sam and Peter returned from town without Oscar.

"We left him there," Sam explained, "He won some money at faro and said he'd be along later." The next day they found the place where Oscar had staggered off the main trail on the river and broke through the rotting springtime ice into waist-deep water. If he had been sober he might have gotten out—they found where he had tried to claw his way back up onto the ice. Pathetic finger scratches in the snow terminated at the edge where Oscar had slid back beneath the cold waters. No one ever found his body. With Oscar gone, John could not bear to stay on Bonanza Creek any longer. Taking the rifle and what he could carry on his meat sled, John gave what was left to Sam and Peter. He pulled the sled down to Dawson, where he bought another gun for shooting birds, and ammunition for the big rifle.

And so John became a professional game hunter, moving from camp to camp down along the river. He lived up to his new name. The miners welcomed him wherever he went, and were eager to buy the moose, caribou, bear and geese he shot. They knew him only as Moose John the hunter, the man who was always alone, and who traveled from camp to camp according to where the game trails led him. He went right past Dawson, downriver to the Fortymile and then to the area around Circle. A few winters later, John was over on the Koyukuk, well north of the Arctic Circle. He hunted back southward to Rampart, then swung eastward to the new camps around Fairbanks, ending up at Ester City.

Even after old Alex had died and left him the mine and cabin, John continued to earn his living by hunting, but he did take a lantern into Alex's tunnel, and there he saw the vein. It was a vertical sheet of quartz extending up along the back of the tunnel from floor to ceiling, and only a few inches wide. Alex had said that you couldn't see the gold, and he was right. Even holding the lantern against the rock, all John could see was soft, brownish quartz laced with metallic-looking sulfides and iron, and on one edge of the vein, bluish-green quartz, hard and barren-looking. Despite Alex's claim about the gold the vein carried, John did not find the mine exciting. He pecked away at the vein with a pick he found lying there in the tunnel, but it was hard work. John soon abandoned the effort.

As time went by, he thought more about the gold and how to get it out. Alex had said to be careful, so John thought he should not talk to anyone about it. Instead, he decided to learn by watching what the other hardrock miners were doing. He stopped by several mines up on the hill above the town and observed the ore being taken out. He saw that the miners threw away all quartz that gleamed white and showed no sign of brown iron and gray sulfides. That was what Alex meant, thought John, you got to save the good stuff, the quartz that carries the gold.

John also went up behind the town to Charley Foster's mill. Trying not to appear too interested, he watched the mill operate, and saw more of the ore that several miners brought there for processing. Seeing that the ore was always brown quartz, with soft streaks of sulfides and reddish brown oxides, John satisfied himself that he knew for sure what he was looking for.

John watched Foster's men shovel the ore into the mouth of the big rock crusher up at the top of the mill structure, a noisy device that shook the ground as it masticated the ore between its steel jaws. He saw the crushed material spew out below into a big, sloping, nearly horizontal drum, slowly rotating and partly filled with steel balls that crushed the ore still finer, almost to a powder. Helped along by a flow of water, the fines emerged in a tiny stream through a hole on the lower end of the drum and ran down through a tube to the shaker table. John could not help becoming excited as he stood beside the table looking down at the thin stream of crushed ore drifting slowly across the table's vibrating surface. The gold-bearing powder came in at the high corner to spread out along the table lengthwise, jumped along by the table's motion back and forth in that direction. Little pebbles and the coarser pieces of crushed sand drifted downslope sideways across the table, aided by water running over the table's surface. The finer and heavier powder stayed behind, but slowly drifted lengthwise. Halfway down the table, the gold started to show. He could see just a few tiny pieces peeking out from the black sand at first, then a gleaming golden streak, widening and standing out from the worthless debris, and stretching down to the far end of the table where it ran off into a big tin bucket. John leaned over the can to see the gold at the bottom, lying several inches deep.

The image of that stream of gold extending down the table and into the pot at the end returned to John's mind as he hurried back home to start digging. A hundred dollars for a bucketful, Alex had said; it had been the first time John had really thought about how it might feel to be rich.

The excitement had paled in proportion to the sweat running down John's forehead as he dug at the vein exposed in the back of the tunnel. He did stay at it long enough to fill two buckets with quartz—although some of the rock in the buckets was just the hard blue-green quartz. Even so, as John cooked his supper that night he figured that he had taken out more than one hundred fifty dollars' worth.

If I could take out two buckets every day, he thought, that would be two hundred dollars. In a month I would have six thousand dollars. That is a fortune. If I worked for most of a year I'd have maybe more than fifty thousand dollars. John was happier than he had been for years when he went to sleep that night.

He continued to dig at the vein during the days ahead. It was hard work, particularly because he had to remove so much worthless rock in order to dig the good stuff. Then too, nearly half of the ore he took out was the hard blue-green quartz. John was careful to sort it out from the rich brown ore each time he emptied his buckets onto the pile he was starting to build. He found it somewhat discouraging that the pile of barren quartz seemed to grow almost as fast as the stack of good ore. Some days, he ended up with barely a bucket of the brown ore, and on some days he got none at all. When the moose started coming down from the hills in the fall, John essentially quit mining altogether. Except for the heavy work of packing out the meat he got, he reaffirmed to himself that hunting was far easier than mining.

John spent as much time thinking and dreaming about being rich as he did digging during that first winter. Progress was very slow. Still, when the snow began to melt in the spring, John had accumulated the beginnings of his fortune. His tally showed that the ore pile he had been building contained seventy buckets of rich brown ore. Seven thousand dollars was there in the pile. That was several times more money than he had made during all the years he'd spent hunting game.

John considered having someone haul his ore pile up to Foster's mill that spring, but argued himself out of the idea. He was making enough money hunting to live, so he didn't need the money now. What would he do with the gold if he milled it out? To keep it safe he'd have to bury it, and then he couldn't look at it. As it was, he could go to the door and peer at it in the pile outside, standing there to think what it meant to his future.

Moose John kept himself happy for six years—mining, hunting and thinking. Then one fall day, as the pungent smells of ripening berries and rotting mushrooms pervaded the woods, John's tally showed that his ore pile contained nine hundred buckets—ninety thousand dollars' worth of gold. That was worthy of celebration, so John went on a long hunting trip, spending several days away. He remembered that trip well. It started out pleasantly, it continued that way, and the end of the trip had begun his new life.

John returned on a late afternoon, walking slowly along the trail with head down and shoulders hunched forward under the heaviness of a boned-out moose in his pack. John's nose picked up the scent of wood smoke wafting up from the settlement as he labored up the last little slope before the trail turned abruptly and led down toward his cabin. Turning the crest, with the sun behind him, John looked up just as his shadow fell across the girl sitting beside the trail picking cranberries. John froze the moment he saw her, amazed by seeing a woman there. Instantly, John accumulated a tumbled sequence of separate little pictures that coalesced in his mind to form one sharp overall image of great beauty. He took in the pert nose framed by full, curving lips, rounded cheeks and dark, wide-set eyes with long black lashes extending out beneath thick arched brows—all of that in turn framed by a full mane of dark brown, almost black, hair extending down the girl's back and parted so that a portion hung over her shoulder and clung to her blouse front. Dainty arms reached below the ruffled sleeves of the white blouse, its fullness just below the shoulder line accentuated by the blouse's tuck into the green skirt encircling a trim waist. The skirt spread out over the ground, except where one stockinged leg extended out toward John, exposed almost to the knee. A beautiful leg it was, with a small foot tightly laced to the ankle in a shiny black shoe. The overall image evoked in John's mind caused a strange feeling to surge through him. It seemed to originate deep in his chest and spread outward and upward into his shoulders.

"Oh, you startled me," the image before John gasped, clasping one pretty arm across her chest.

She turned quickly to face him, her knee striking her berry bucket and spilling its contents across the moss. She recovered quickly, and a broad smile of relief spread across her face. "Now look what I've done," she exclaimed, in a voice that was surprisingly deep and musical. That voice, trilling out into the little surrounding glen, brought new life to the bushes and trees standing there in the sunshine, giving John a sense of the place having a great beauty that he had never before recognized.

"Oh...I'm...sorry," John stammered. He had not used his voice for several days, but that was not the only reason his words came out haltingly. "I'll help you pick up the berries." He slid his pack off and knelt down beside her, his hands clumsy as he began scooping up the red cranberries. Seeing his fingers, he became conscious of their roughness and the dried moose blood caught beneath the nails. He wished now that he had cleaned them earlier.

"My name is Mary Ellen; I work down at the Malemute Saloon. What's yours?"

"I'm John, Moose John."

"Oh yes, I've heard of you. You are the hunter. They say that you are always able to get meat, even when nobody else can find anything." John was embarrassed but pleased with the compliment. He wanted very much to look up at Mary Ellen's face, to take in the sight of those lovely dark eyes, but he was too shy to do so. He kept his head bowed, looking only at his and her hands picking up the last of the scattered berries. When the task was complete, Mary Ellen said, "Thank you very much, John, for helping me. I think I should go home now. I'll walk with you down the trail."

John shouldered his pack and followed her along, trying hard not to look at the curves of her body, but letting himself anyway. He felt very alive. Despite the weight on his back, he stepped lightly, rising up off the balls of his feet with each stride. As they approached John's cabin, Mary Ellen said, "I'm pleased to have met you, John. I hope I will see you again."

"Yes, I'm sorry I made you spill your berries." John wanted to say more, but did not know what else to say. With regret, he watched her head on down the trail toward the town below.

Full of excitement, John hung the meat he had carried in, prepared his supper and ate it, hardly aware of what he was doing. Then he walked back up the trail to the spot where he had met Mary Ellen. He stood in the little glen and conjured up her image again. He could see every detail and hear her say, "Now look what I've done." John bent down near where she had sat, noting a little furrow in the ground where her shoe had scraped toward the trail. He could see the pressed-down moss where she sat. He smelled her presence, saw her fingers searching out the spilled berries and heard her laughter. Reaching down, he picked up a small frond of dark-green cranberry leaves, its stem broken off by some part of her body. Carrying it back home, he vowed right then to marry Mary Ellen.

Back at the cabin, John stood before the ore pile to tote up its value. Not enough. Ninety thousand dollars was a lot of money, but not enough for him and Mary Ellen together. John picked up his two buckets and entered the tunnel. By late evening he had filled them both, having worked at a frenzied pace, faster than ever before. He went to bed very happy that night, looking again at the cranberry leaves he had pressed into a magazine before blowing out the lamp.

John dug and picked away steadily until midafternoon of the next day. Telling himself that he needed groceries anyway, he washed up in preparation to going down into Ester City. John strolled slowly past the homes of people he did not know, hoping to learn which was Mary Ellen's. He went to the Malemute where he saw only a few men playing cards in the rear. No Mary Ellen. In a sense he was relieved at not finding her. He really did not want to see her there in the saloon, nor could he bring himself to ask the bartender where she lived. Back outside, John wandered around the town, trying to look as if he had some important purpose. No luck, so he went back home until darkness came.

The central part of the town was alive with voices, laughter and music when he approached the Malemute again. He stopped outside, peering in over the curving tops of the swinging doors. Smoke and the dank odor of wet sawdust and whiskey seeped out toward him. He did not like the smell. There she was! He saw Mary Ellen, leaning over a table of men, her dark hair tied up around her head, her shoulders bare above the flaring red dress that barely came below her knees. One of the men had his arm around her waist as she talked to him. John turned away, brooding as he walked back to his cabin. I'll take her out of there, he thought. She should not be in a place like that.

Several days passed before John got up nerve to go into Ester again. No more luck this time, but several days later he saw Mary Ellen turn into the mercantile down the boardwalk ahead of him. He hurried to the door to wait for her, then became self-conscious about standing there like that and moved on down the street. His heart sank when he saw her emerge chatting with two other women. He could not approach her with them there, so he followed behind down the street, keeping well back to avoid their becoming aware of him. Mary Ellen turned into one of the little cabins, all alike, standing side by side just beyond the Malemute, and the two women went to others nearby. Finally John had learned where Mary Ellen lived! He started toward her door, then suddenly panicked, feeling unsure of what to say when she would come to the door at his knock. Later, he thought, turning away.

So it went for weeks. John walked to Ester City frequently during the afternoons, when he thought Mary Ellen might be about on the streets. He saw her several times, always some distance away or with someone else, never approachably alone. Then he failed to see her at all for several days, though by now he knew her habits and when she should be out shopping. He decided to go back to the saloon one night, dreading the thought of doing so, but feeling he had to see her. The room was full of men and women—but no Mary Ellen. He went in.

"Whiskey," John told the bartender, ordering the first drink of his life.

"This one's on us. House policy, mister; always good to see a new customer," said the bartender as he set the shot glass on the bar before John.

"Say, that dark-haired girl, Mary Ellen, where's she?"

"Oh, yeah. Everybody's been asking about her. Went Outside to visit her poor old sick mother in Indiana. But don't worry, mister, she'll be back. Sometime after Christmas, she said. Well, cheers."

Thus John's courtship of Mary Ellen was long delayed. He fretted that she might not return, and he cursed himself because he had failed to accost her before she left. In the meantime, he worked hard in the mine and also hunted vigorously in order to build up his meager money supply. Despite his frenetic activity, John felt distraught and empty all the while Mary Ellen was gone. The fear that he might never see her again made it difficult to think about his hoped-for future with her. After Christmas passed, John made almost daily trips into Ester to see if she was back. It was a great relief when she did finally return in late January, allowing John the chance to begin his courtship and pursue his other activities with the pleasure of knowing that they were, once more, worth pursuing.

John was sorely tempted all that spring to tell Mary Ellen about the gold. However, he kept the matter entirely to himself while rehearsing for the telling, and also the actual marriage proposal. He decided to do it all on the day he had one hundred thousand dollars' worth of ore in the pile and had its gold extracted up at Foster's mill. And John decided he must look his best for the grand event. One day he walked into Fairbanks with his poke and bought the suit, the hat and the new shoes. Not ever having purchased a suit before, John was uneasy about the whole affair. He walked up and down the street in front of the haberdashery several times before going in, fearful that once inside he might not know what to say, or that he would suffer the embarrassment of discovering that the store might not have a suit big enough for him.

It was awkward at first, John standing there dressed in his rough clothes before the salesman, blurting out that he wanted to buy a good suit, but the man was very nice, and the experience finally was almost pleasurable. In fact, the store did have only two suits that even came close to fitting John, and both were tight about his shoulders. He and the salesman picked the dark blue one, and while the seamstress let it out they selected the hat, the shoes and a shirt. Within three hours John had it all in his pack and was jauntily walking back to Ester City, feeling already rich, even though his poke now contained little more than one hundred dollars in gold.

John knew he looked dapper in the new outfit, but Mary Ellen was not going to see it until the time when he proposed to her. He could imagine the expression on her face as he reached into the suit pocket to take out a hefty sample of the gold Foster had milled out. "Look at this, Mary Ellen," he would say, and spread the contents of the poke across her table. "There's a lot more, too. A hundred thousand dollars' worth, and when people find out how much gold there is in my mine they will be willing to pay big money to buy it—maybe even another hundred thousand dollars." Yes, that is the way he would do it, and now he was almost ready. Just a few more days of digging to be done.

The leaves were just coming out on the trees when John fulfilled his goal. Adding the last bucket of ore to the now-huge pile was not as much fun as John thought it would be. He stood there for a while thinking, then ate a quick noontime meal and headed off to Foster's mill.

"Hello, Moose John, haven't seen you for quite a while. How have you been?"

"Fine, Mr. Foster, fine. Say, I got a big milling job for you. Want you to haul my ore up here and get the gold out." Now that he had made the big decision, John was like a man running downhill. He could not pause or digress into the circuitous discussion that normally accompanied any miner's transaction. "How soon?" he continued.

"Well, how about that. Yes, I heard you been stocking up a bit of ore. How much you got down there, John?"

"A lot, Mr. Foster, I got a lot of ore—maybe ten wagons full; maybe even more."

"O.K., John. I reckon we can do it. Be a few days

before we can start 'cause we got to finish this run for Charley Jackson first. Guess we could start hauling tomorrow. I charge ten dollars a ton for milling, and we will haul it for another five."

"Fine, I'll be ready tomorrow."

John was waiting impatiently when the two horse-drawn wagons arrived the next morning, driven by two young men. With much bantering between them, the two brought the first wagon to John's pile and began shoveling in ore. They worked slowly, it seemed to John, so before long he had a shovel in hand and was scooping away beside them. It felt good, and soon the first wagon was full, with John having loaded nearly as much ore as the other two together. John suspected that the boys were intentionally slowing down and laughing secretly about his doing so much of their assigned work. He didn't care; he was rich and they were not. Now he only had to work if he wanted to.

Even with John's help, it took three days to haul all the ore to Foster's mill. John went up with the last two wagons, knowing that the milling would not have started yet, but just to see the pile that now was ready to go into the mill.

"It's going to be another day or two before we start, John," Foster said. "We had a little breakdown yesterday, but we about got it fixed. We'll start day after tomorrow on yours. You sure got a bunch here, John. It's gonna take us three days to do it." John was disappointed at that news. Nothing to do about it, so he went back home. He thought briefly about going to see Mary Ellen that evening. Yet he knew she would be at work in the Malemute, and he was not in a mood to share her with the boisterous crowd in the saloon.

At home, John found himself with nothing to do, no way to rid himself of restlessness. He packed some food and a blanket in his pack, took down his big rifle, and headed up the trail. He stopped at the little glen where he first met Mary Ellen, now a consecrated place in John's mind. He saw her sitting there, the black hair trailing down her back, her hand clutched across her breast, and the berries spilling out of the little bucket. The memory seemed almost painful, so he walked quickly on.

John headed uphill to the ridgetop and followed along it to the west, mile after mile, through open groves of aspen, birch and spruce, unmindful of fresh moose tracks encountered or of squirrels that chattered at him as he passed. Eventually John came to a crest where the ridge stuck out to the south. Here, he could look out over the braided Tanana River, miles away and far below. Its main channel came up against the base of the upland mass on which John stood, then looped out in great curving arcs into the flat country beyond, only to swing back and deflect off the hills again. For fifty miles it skirted the hills in that fashion and then disappeared out of view where it swung northward to flow toward its juncture with the Yukon, another hundred miles away.

In the distance, toward the southwest, far beyond the broad valley floor, John could see the foothills of the Alaska Range, green and brown at the bottom and trending into the snowy whiteness of the high mountains beyond, mountains so far away that only their tops were visible. In all that space between John and the mountains, no sign of human occupation showed, nor any hint that man had ever crossed. Nor did the sign of people appear anywhere as John's eyes swept leftward over the expanse of the valley until he was looking up toward the Tanana's headwaters, with another hundred-mile stretch in view. John was alone with the valley, its hills, and the great arc of mountains following along the visible curve of the earth.

The long walk up to the viewpoint had relaxed John, and now he felt very tired. He wrapped himself in his blanket and lay down on his packboard until he went to sleep, just as the last red glow of the sun left the peaks to the south. When he awoke, the sun had wheeled around behind his back, just below the horizon, and was rising again in the northeast. John spent the entire day sitting there thinking a turmoil of thoughts, happy ones about the future laced occasionally with curiously uneasy remembrances of the past that he was ready to cast behind him as soon as Foster finished milling the ore.

Toward the end of that day, he thought about heading back to Ester. Instead, John shouldered his pack and, for some reason that he did not understand, followed the beckoning westward trail.

He walked all night, slept a few hours, then continued west along the ridges. He finally came to ground he had never walked before. By now, he thought, Foster would be starting to mill the ore, and John's gold would be running off the shaker table into the tin bucket at its end. John continued on westward, wondering how many pokes it would take to hold a hundred thousand dollars in gold. He mulled over that for some miles, imagining what the gold would look like and if he would be able to carry it all at once. Probably not, he decided; he might have to make several trips to Foster's mill to get it all.

John walked until the ridge terminated, and he could see the river where it curved northward around the base of the last hill and ran across the flats in a narrowing silver-brown streak toward the hills beyond. He stood there briefly, then whirled and began the trip back, walking rapidly while his thoughts focused on the gold and Mary Ellen. John tried to rehearse the proposal, over and over, but found it difficult to run through from beginning to end. No matter, he now knew the words by heart, and he let his mind ramble jerkily from thought to disconnected thought.

Unmindful of the hours and the miles, John hurried back along the ridge. Halfway to Ester City, he lay down and slept fitfully for a time. Then he was up and hurrying on. As at last he approached his cabin, John realized that he had been gone nearly four days. All of the gold would be ready now.

John started his fire, cooked a meal and washed himself carefully, more carefully than he had in years. He put on the new suit, the new shoes and the new hat, spending much time before his little mirror to set it in place just the right way. Finally, he took out his poke, emptied it into a can, and folded the worn leather bag into the pocket of his suit.

John had planned this moment well, and now he carried out his scheme. Instead of taking the short trail over the hill to Foster's mill, John walked the long way down through Ester City. It was late afternoon; not many people were about. Enough, though, to make John feel good as they saw him stride importantly down the street. John chuckled to himself as he walked along. Sure bet they are surprised to see me all dressed up. Wait until they hear the news; then they will know why. He then realized that he might meet Mary Ellen on the street, a thought that had not occurred to him before. Not wanting that to happen, John walked quickly on, daring not even a glance at her house as he went past. He was greatly relieved when he got through the town and was striding up the hill to Foster's mill.

John was almost running when he got there. He noticed that the mill was silent. A good sign, that; it meant that they had his gold ready. He saw Mr. Foster sitting in his little office attached to the mill, so John went in through the open door.

"Here I am, Mr. Foster. I c-c-come to get my gold," John stammered.

Foster looked up, then settled back in his chair to light his pipe. "Well, John...Hmm...I hate to tell you this, but that ore of yours really didn't have much in it. Fact is, John, there was not enough there to pay for the milling. You still owe me eighty dollars. Surprised you would bring me ore like that. You must ᶦnot have been sampling it as you went along. Hard to understand. I'm sure sorry."

Even as Foster had started to settle back in his chair, John had sensed the terrible feeling that something was wrong. He was so stunned that he barely heard the fateful words. John stood there, slumped down in his new suit. Eventually he said, "I ain't got the money with me. It's down at the cabin." He paused a long while, then said, "Mr. Foster, would you mind coming down to my cabin tomorrow to get it?"

"Why sure, John. Man's had a little bad luck, I don't mind going out of my way to get paid. I'll be there in the morning."

The next day, after Windy Barnes, one of Foster's men, first told the story down at the Malemute, John's misfortune was the talk of the camp. "Yessir, boys," Windy had said, taking a snort on his glass and looking around the room to make sure that everyone was listening, "that was really sumpthin'. That crazy guy spent all those years working in Alex Vladovich's mine, and he had a big pile of ore, too. Brought it up to the mill, and there weren't hardly any value in it. Worked all those years for nothin', he did. And when Mr. Foster and me went down to his cabin this morning to get paid the money he owed, ole Moose John was sittin' slumped over his table with the money in front of him and his brains all over the wall behind. He was all dressed up in his new suit, like he was going to a dance or sumpthin', but he sure was deader than hell." Windy paused for effect—and to take another drink. "Shot hisself in the head with that big gun of his. All for nothin' too, 'cause he was a rich man.

"That's right, boys, he was rich. Outside his cabin was a big pile of the blue-green quartz you sometimes find hereabouts. The stuff with lotsa gold in it. I ain't never seen it before, but Mr. Foster recognized it right off. We ground up some of that rock and panned it out right there beside Moose's cabin. By God, it was rich! Must have been near an ounce of gold in that pan, and it weren't much rock either. Sure is a pity, ain't it, boys, that a man would make such a mistake?"

"That's really too bad," one of the ladies said, "Poor man. I met him once when I was picking berries up behind his cabin, and he walked a ways back with me. Real shy, he was, and didn't talk much. Saw him walking along the street some after that, but I never spoke with him again."

And so that is the miner's tale of Moose John. If you didn't believe it, maybe you should have—because that is exactly how John died in his cabin near that beautiful little knoll up behind Ester City. But if you did accept the story as truth, perhaps you shouldn't have, because only Moose John really knew his own thoughts.

※　※　※

Willy's Undoing

The thing you need to know about my partner Willy was that he was awful finicky, and he sure had a sensitive nose. Except for the troubles that caused, Willy was real good to be around, and we'd prospected together the better part of ten years, ever since we first met near Dawson. We'd wandered a lot of creeks together in the summers, and wintered over in cabins we found or sometimes built.

Willy's real name was Wilfred Winchester Wilkensfield, III, but of course nobody knew that except me, and he never told even me how he got such a strange long handle. Me and everybody else just called him Willy. During the years he was my partner, I never really figured him out, but he was the best partner I ever had, that's for sure. I owed Willy a lot 'cause I was sick as a dog when we first met. He found me pretty near dead in a tent alongside the trail, and he'd stayed there with me and fed me until I could walk again. We started being partners then.

I don't know why Willy came north to Dawson

from back where he lived near Seattle. Had he stayed there, I think he would have become a scientist or an engineer or something like that, instead of just a prospector like me. Willy knew a lot, he thought a lot, and he looked like a guy who ought to be wearing glasses on his long, sorta elegant-like nose. I'm not sure how far Willy went in school, but it was far more than me. So's I could work more, Pa made me quit even before I learned to read and write real good. But I figure Willy must have been in a college, because he sure was smart, even if he was peculiar. One thing I admired about him right off was some of the fancy words he could use. He had to tell me the meanings of some of them, but after being around Willy for a while I got so's I could say lots of them pretty darn good. I figure one reason Willy enjoyed having me around was that he liked to learn people things, and I was such a good learner.

Odd thing about Willy was that he always seemed nervous and wanting to keep himself busy all the time. He talked in his sleep a lot. I figure he had bad dreams, too, because sometimes he'd be mumbling things I couldn't understand, then call out "bad" or "Mommy" and suddenly sit up with his eyes open. He'd fall right back down again without even waking up. Things like that didn't bother me none, and I didn't even tell Willy he was doing it. Willy was peculiar in other ways that hinged mostly around his being so particular about eating and wanting to be clean all the time. Like he used to carry an extra bag of salt along so's he could put some on one of his long, skinny fingers and rub his teeth with it, every single day, morning and night. He even washed himself all over every day or so, and his face and hands two or three times. Seems like he was always washing clothes, too. He washed them so much they wore out a lot faster than mine. I reckon he'd go through three pants and shirts for every set I needed.

When you are out on the creeks like we was, I always figured there was little sense to washing up too often. I'd do it more than I wanted to, though, just because of Willy. Willy never said nothing, we being such good partners and all, but when I'd notice his nose twitching if he was up close to me, I'd wash up my gear, too. Seems like that happened nearly every month or so during the summer, and even more often when we was holed up in a winter cabin somewhere.

Sometimes Willy's persnickety ways were bothersome. Like that time six years ago December when we were out on the trail all day packing in a moose. We got so tired we couldn't make the cabin that night, and had to camp out up on a hill after dark. While Willy got a fire going, I collected snow to melt in our coffee pot. The snow was real dry, so it took me most of an hour to get the pot filled with hot water. Then Willy looked down into it and saw that the top of the water was covered with a thick layer of rabbit turds. I wanted to just scoop them off and drink the water anyway, but Willy wouldn't go for it. I had to spend another hour doing the whole thing all over again. This time, I made sure I wasn't collecting any turds at all. I told Willy I thought he was being powerful fussy, but he said he wasn't fussy at all, just nacherally fastiderous.

Willy caused me all sorts of extra work like that, especially since we shared alike in the cooking, and I figured I had to do it his way. You always got to treat your partner good if you want him to keep on being your partner. So I always had to clean any bits of hair and dirt off the moose meat before cooking it, and that could take a lot of time. That was nothing, though, compared to the hours I spent washing dishes. Willy thought they ought to be washed every time we used them. It's easier and quicker just to wipe them off with moss, and mostly they don't even need that. But that's Willy for you, always wanting everything so dadblamed clean and neat. I tell you all this because it's what made the thing that happened to Willy two years ago last fall so bad for him, and I can't say as I enjoyed it too much either.

Willy and me had been out prospecting all summer without finding anything. Part of the trouble was, early on, we'd run into a moose calf that had got caught in a downed tree and broke his leg. His mother had run off, and just as we came up a wolf was about ready to start eating the calf. I had in mind eating him myself, but after we chased the wolf off, Willy went and fixed up a splint on that calf's leg. Worse yet, he insisted that we prospect close by until the critter could make it on his own. Never thought I'd end up spending the better part of a month cutting willows for a busted moose and panning a creek any dang fool could see carried no gold. Staying there taking care of that moose sure cut into our serious prospecting time, and that was pretty much why Willy and me was not doing well so far that summer.

After the moose finally ran off over the hill one day, we managed to pan a few ounces out of some of the gravel bars along the Kanuti. Still, we was facing a pretty slim winter if we didn't find something better soon. We was almost out of grub, too, and Willy had worn out his last set of clothes. I gave him my one extra set, and he was wearing them when we dropped over into another valley to the south. It was part of the Tazitna, I learned later when we followed it down to the Yukon.

We hit that valley about halfway up and started finding colors right away in the bars of its little river. No rich pans, but it was looking good enough that we kept right on panning up the valley. The pans got better as we went along, but then the pay quit. We was seeing no gold at all for about a mile, so we turned around and panned back downstream, trying to find where the gold was coming from. It was a real puzzlement, 'cause we didn't see any side valleys that could be feeding the gold into the main one we was following.

When we finally found the right place, Willy and me figured out why we had missed it going up. The little river was running right alongside a cliff there, and down at the base of that cliff we hit rich pay in the side gravels, in a strip that was little more than ten feet wide. Just above the pay, the cliff was frozen mucks, but to each side it was solid rock. Looking things over real close, we saw what had happened. A long time ago, a little side valley only a few feet wide used to open up right into the stream. Now it was all plugged up with frozen muck so that it didn't even look like a valley coming in. After we climbed up on top, about fifty feet up from the stream, Willy and me could see that sometime a big mudslide had plugged up the little gulch where we found the gold. There on top of the slide, we found where the water coming down from the hills above was ponded up into a little puddle that drained over its side and on down the hill behind the cliff. It came out to the river about a hundred paces downstream. We had seen that trickle of water when we was panning upstream the first time and had looked enough there to know that the gold was not coming out into the valley there.

Willy and me figured we was pretty lucky to find the place. We knew that at least one other prospector had looked in this valley within the last few years because we found a tin can down a few miles. We pondered a little over why he hadn't found the paystreak like we had, but not much, because we'd walked right past too the first time without taking much notice of all that moss and muck in between the rock walls. I hadn't seen it at all, but I remember that as we walked past that first time, Willy's nose had twitched a little and he had said, "Smells just like sour horse piss around here." It did, too. After Willy's remark I could smell it some, but then we had gone on.

After coming back down the stream, we took a few pans out from the gravel below the mucks, and we knew we had hit it good. Willy and me did not even have to talk about it; we knew we was going to set up right there and work as long as we could. We'd both been hankering to spend a winter in one of the camps, maybe Ruby, Tanana or even Manley Hot Springs, and it looked like we'd get enough gold here in just a few weeks to winter over in the comfort of a nice town cabin, maybe even staying in a hotel if we found enough gold.

Of course we had to get ourselves organized first. I set up our tent on the bank just a little ways downstream from the paystreak. While I was doing that, Willy used his axe to cut what pieces he needed to finish up the little shaker box we used when we found enough gold for it to be worthwhile. We carried with us most of the main parts: canvas, screen boxes to keep the bigger gravels off the riffle, and the riffle box itself. Willy only had to make up some of the frame and rocker pieces and put the thing together. He was so good at this kind of work that he had it all finished by the time I had camp set up. Then we went hunting and Willy dropped a right sizable bull moose with one shot only about a half mile upstream. We had all the meat we could eat in a month back at the tent before dark.

The next day we were hard at it in the gravels sticking out below the muck. By gosh, it was fun! Willy and me was both pretty excited from being able to pick up nuggets out of the head of the shaker box—one was bigger than the end of my thumb. We had better than a thousand dollars' worth by the end of the third day. That was enough to winter over on, but of course we was not about to quit then, not with all that gold lying there in that bank.

Lucky for Willy and me, the gold-bearing gravel was thawed. I guess it was because of the water from the river seeping in there all the time, but the muck on top was frozen solid just a few inches up above the gravel. That part of the dirt facing out toward the river was thawed, too, back in about three feet. Willy and me could see we was going to have a lot of trouble with that thawed muck sluffing down on us as we tunneled in underneath it. So we cut a few trees down and built a log frame to hold up the loose dirt, and that worked pretty well.

We did have some trouble, though, as we dug farther in, 'cause some of the muck was melting above the top of our cut into the gravel. The thawed muck started dripping down on us while we worked. That was nasty, but the worst thing was that it smelled so bad. The odor Willy had noticed when we walked past that first day was getting worse all the time. It was a sort of half sweet, half acidy smell like what Willy had said, "sour horse piss." Fastiderous as he was, Willy used language like that an awful lot, the kinds of things you'd never say if you was around a woman. It was funny to hear Willy mix in those kinds of words with all the fancy ones he knew.

One morning when we went over to begin work we saw that several inches of thawed muck had fallen down, and it smelled real bad. Willy went in the cut to start cleaning it up, but almost right away staggered out looking real pale. He threw up over by the stream, and he was so weak then that he just sat down and watched while I cleaned out the cut. I could understand why it bothered Willy so. Far back in the cut, the smell was real powerful. It could gag a maggot. I was glad I had such a strong stomach or I might have woofed up just like Willy did.

If we'd had enough head room, we could have timbered up the top of the cut to keep all that muck from melting and falling down on us. Willy and me talked about it, but we realized that we had to let about three feet of the muck melt off first so's we'd have enough room to work. The gold-bearing gravel was only about two feet thick, and it was resting on solid rock. The pay was so good there on the rock surface that Willy and me was sweeping it real clean with some little brooms we'd made out of willow twigs and blueberry bushes all tied together. We was sweeping down the two rock walls, too, to get the gold off them. Those walls were about ten feet apart on the face of the cliff, and they seemed to be getting closer the farther in we dug. Right at the back of the cut, the walls were only about six feet apart, and nearly straight up and down. Willy and me could see that this must have been a pretty spectacular little gulch before it got plugged up with all this mucky crap. If it kept going like this, the walls were going to pinch down to nothing, but since all the gold was laying in there, we knew that wouldn't happen. That gold had washed in there from the hills up above, and it could have done that only if the gulch was open a long time ago.

Willy and me was having more trouble with the muck as we went along. As soon as enough of it thawed near the front to give us working room, we put in new timbers behind the ones already there. After about a week, we had what looked like a log-roofed room about ten feet long, sloping down toward the back end of the cut to where it was about three feet above the rock floor of the little gulch. We kept reaching in under the muck as far as we could to pull the gravel out, and the pay was staying good. By now we had better'n three thousand dollars' worth of gold, and was feeling rich. Willy, though, was getting awful skinny from up-chucking so much. Suppers were the only meals he could keep down.

Willy was all for quitting early that fall. "I'm gettin' awful goddamn tired of this smell and eating nothin' but moose meat," he moaned one evening. "We've got plenty of money already. Let's go into Manley and stay there for the winter. We can come out next year, and maybe bring along an Indian to help with the mining so's I don't have to go into that miserable goddamn place again."

I was doing my best to argue him into staying on for another few weeks. "Willy, maybe this is just a little pocket that we can work out by then and not have to come back at all," I suggested. Willy could see that my idea was right meritorious. Despite his troubles with the bad smells in the muck, he enjoyed as much as me seeing all that gold come out of the ground. And of course since I'd been such a good partner to him, Willy didn't like to go against what I

wanted to do.

"Yeah, I suppose we could stay a little longer," he agreed, not real happy-like, "but I sure wish that muck would thaw faster so we could get down in there to get more pay dirt out." Willy poured himself another cup of Labrador tea—that being the only thing we had to drink any more. He reached daintily into his cup with a spoon to flick out a twig that I'd dropped in by mistake when I'd picked the leaves over across the stream. Then Willy got that far-away look in his eyes like he gets when he's real tribulated.

"What we need," he said finally, "is a fire."

I could see what he was thinking about. Over in the Iditarod region, Willy and me had once sunk a shaft down through frozen ground more than fifty feet deep. Why Willy was thinking in that direction escaped me, though, because that's an awful slow way to put a hole down. We'd built a fire in the bottom of the shaft and let it go out, then hoist out the dirt that had thawed before building another fire. Never got more than a foot every two days, and it sure was a heck of a lot of work cutting all that wood. Turned out that when we got down to the gravel after a couple of months, it was barren, so the whole thing was wasted effort. After that, Willy and me stuck to panning the river bars.

I didn't say nothing, 'cause I could see that Willy was cogitating real hard. He was good at figuring things out, so I knew it would be good to let him sit there and ponder over it for a while.

I was right. Pretty soon Willy's eyes lit up. "Yup, a fire," he says, "one helluva fire. But we're gonna

need a chimney. Got to figure out how to do that."
Willy walked over to the stream, and hunkered
down to wash his hands for the third time that
evening. His eyes gazed upstream where he saw a
jumbled pile of sheet-like rocks that had slid down
from the cliff there.

"I got it," Willy says, and he went on to tell me his
plan. Up above our timbering, we would dig a hole
down from the face of the muck and line it with flat
rocks. From where the hole came down to the top of
the timbering we would have to slide rocks in up
over the timbers and prop them together to make a
sort of horizontal chimney extending all the way
back past the timbering into the top of the cut.

"We're gonna make just one big fire in there and
let it burn for a few days, real slow-like. It should
melt that muck back maybe five feet or even a lot
more. After the fire's out, we'll dig the thawed muck
away and take out as much gravel as we can. Then
we quit and go into Manley for the winter. What do
you think of that proposition?"

I wasn't sure how well all this was going to come
out, but I figured that if Willy was game to hang on
for a couple more weeks I'd go along with him on it.
The thing that was bothering me was that I suspected Willy's big fire would not last long because
when the muck above it began to melt, it would fall
down and put the fire out.

Willy had that one figured out, too, I discovered
after we got the two chimney sections built. We
brought in a whole bunch of dry wood and laid it in
the back of the cut between two stacks of flat rocks.

Across those rocks we laid fresh-cut black spruce logs up to six inches across. That made a sort of a firebox about six feet long which came up from the floor to the frozen muck at the top of the cut. We managed to wedge in three layers of those green logs above the rocks, and we cut notches in them for smoke passages. Willy then had me cut a whole bunch more shorter pieces of green spruce that we propped on end across most of the front of the firebox so that their ends jammed against the floor and ceiling. We put in more than ten layers of those, leaving a narrow space coming out to the front of the cut so's we could light the fire and shove more dry wood in if need be.

I got to admit that when we got done, we had one heck of an impressive stack of wood in the cut, all neatly arranged like Willy wanted. The challenge of getting it all done right titillerated him so much that his weak stomach barely bothered him—he only threw up twice in three days. 'Course the horse pee smell got weaker the more wood we piled into the cut, and I couldn't even hardly smell it at all after we piled dirt up around the last of the green logs.

"Hot damn, she's going well," Willy said after he lit some birch bark and shoved it in through the tunnel to get it under the dry wood. Pretty soon, we had a right toasty fire going in there, and smoke was boiling up out of our chimney. It was burning so well that Willy had me lay some sticks across the top of the chimney to cut down the draft. "We got to keep her going a long time; she needs to burn real slow and easy like," he said.

Willy is the kind who thinks ahead, so he had used his axe to whittle some boards for a pair of bellows. He had to cut a strip of canvas off the bottom of our tent to finish them up. That didn't matter 'cause we'd already shortened that tent up so much from taking material off for other purposes that it was time for a new one. The tent was getting dingy too, so I knew Willy would insist on buying a new one anyway, now that we had plenty of money.

But the fire went so well that Willy never even put the bellows to it once. It was going far better than he had planned on, as we could tell every time we peeked in to see a nice deep red glow in the back of the cut. Willy and me spent the next few days just laying around, picking blueberries and even doing a little fishing. That fire burned for near onto a week, and Willy figured we ought to wait another two days before we dug it out.

About the time the red glow died away to nothing, Willy's nose began to twitch badly, and even I noticed a peculiar smell near the opening of the cut. It was still sort of horse-pissy, but somehow a lot worse. Trying to figure out what it was, Willy took one good breath, and of course you know what happened then.

When we began pulling the dirt away from the front of our fire, I sure was surprised to find some of those green logs in there still smoldering away. So far, not much of the thawed muck in the roof had fallen, but the smell back there in the cut sure was powerful bad. Willy was having such a terrible time with it that I offered to dig the place out, and Willy agreed. He went right over to the stream and washed himself off, including his shirt, pants and long johns, while I continued to work.

As I got back in near the end of our cut, I noticed something awful strange, and I could see why not much of the thawed muck had fallen in on the fire. That stuff just stayed up there because it seemed to be stuck together with something that looked like fine brown roots. I had no idea what they were, but they was doing such a good job of holding the roof up that I figured I'd better clean out the rest of the muck, and just leave the ceiling alone until the very end.

It was while I was digging away at the back corner of the cut, right up against the left wall, when I came to what looked something like an elephant's foot resting right on top of the gravel. Must be a log, I thought, but I dug up a little higher, and I heard a little "whoof" as a whole bunch of muck fell away. Heck, it is an elephant's foot! I sez to myself when I sees that the foot was attached to a big leg, and that over to the right was another one sort of folded over like it was broke. Up above the break, enough muck had fallen away that I could see what looked like more of the leg with its knee jammed over against the rock wall to the right.

I come running out of the cut yelling, "Willy, Willy, you got to come see this. I found an elephant!" Willy didn't answer, and I guessed he'd gone off for a walk or to pick some more berries. I was so excited I goes back in the cut to dig and look around some more.

I studied them two legs sticking down, and it looked to me like they was front legs, although I wasn't sure because I'd only seen an elephant once when I was a kid and went to a circus. Seeing how those legs was pointed, it occurred to me that if the rest of the elephant was there, the critter was right up on top of me in the muck. I looked up at the ceiling and again saw the muck entangled in the roots I had seen earlier, but it wasn't quite like roots. "Gotta be elephant hair," I sez to myself, and I got my knife out for some exploratory digging. I poked up about six inches before I comes to the elephant's belly. The light was bad in there, but I could see that the belly was like hard leather, sort of shiny and blue-brown. With my fingers I could pull away big clumps of elephant hair and thawed muck. By golly, I tell you, it was pretty dang exciting, even if the smell in there was getting worse.

I worked fast, and before long I had uncovered a big strip of that elephant more than an arm's length wide and twice as long. Never having seen an elephant's belly up so close, I sure couldn't get over how smooth and round it was. I could have been looking up at a big iron water tank laid on its side. When I chipped away some more muck and hair out toward the timbered part of the cut, I came to something I never in my life expected to see from such a perspective. Gawd Almighty, it was a man elephant! It surely was.

Just then, I hears Willy come walking up to the cut. I runs outside and right up to him, and he turns his head aside like he wants to breathe over his shoulder. "Come in here, Willy, you gotta see something," I sez. "I ain't gonna tell you what it is 'cause you won't believe it." I grabs Willy's hand and drags him into the cut, while he pinches his nose with the fingers of his other hand.

I tell you, Willy was stunned at what he saw. "Holy Jumpin' Christ! It's the belly of a woolly mammoth," he almost hollered.

"Oh, I thought it was an elephant," I said, real disappointed that I hadn't found one after all. But I could tell from the way that Willy was looking around that he thought I'd found something pretty unusual.

"Migawd, the whole thing's preserved—hair, skin and all," Willy said in an awed tone. "Must be ten thousand years old, or more than that." Glancing up over his head, Willy continued, "He must have gotten carried in here in the mudslide and been jammed in between the walls of this little valley. Poor bugger broke his leg, too, just like that little moose, and he's been frozen in ever since."

Willy seemed to have forgotten all about the smell there in the cut. He was so excited he was almost jumping up and down. I wasn't exactly sure what he was talking about when he says something like, "Fantastic...incredible...sonofabitch. It's like we've suddenly been transmortified back into the Pleistocene. Nobody I ever heard of has seen an entire woolly mammoth before." Willy was so happy I was starting not to mind that I'd found a mammoth instead of an elephant.

I sure admired Willy for knowing so much and

being such a thinker. Willy was the best partner I
ever had, that's for certain. Standing there beside
him I purely got caught up in his thinking about
things and his wanting to know more. So I takes out
my knife again and sticks it up against the tight skin
on the belly of the mammoth. "This stuff sure is
tough," I said, "I wonder how thick it is."

"Oh, Jesus, don't do th....," and them was the last
sensible words I ever heard from my partner Willy.

A gawd-awful sort of whooshy explosion muffled
Willy's voice, and the whole dang world fell in on us.
The next thing I knew, Willy and me was sitting
there on the floor of the cut, up to our armpits in a
warm slime of real putrid mammoth insides. Over
Willy's shoulder draped the biggest dang gut I ever
saw. Willy's head sort of sagged over against it as he
passed out from the terrible smell.

I was feeling more than a little faint myself. Oh
boy, it was bad! I just ain't got the words to describe
the overpowering stink there in the cut. If you put together the ripe stench of a full outhouse in late summer with the fetid smell of a bloated dead horse just
opened by vultures, and then threw in the reek of
rotten eggs, plus maybe a few good cabbage farts,
you'd be halfway to the odor pressing in on us. You
could smell it, and you could even taste it on your
tongue and all over the inside of your mouth.

I knew I had to get Willy out of there quick.
Looking down, I sees another big slimy mammoth
bowel lying right across my lap. I raises one knee,
trying to get up, when that gut busts wide open,
flooding my legs with a thick brown soup even more

odiferous than what I am already smelling. Staggering to my feet, I untangles Willy from the mess he is in and I drags him out of there. Just in time, too, 'cause most of the skeleton of that mammoth soon comes crashing down to make a big heap of bones right where Willy and me was sitting.

Soon as Willy comes to, he starts screaming, and he runs over to the stream and throws himself in, head and all. I figure he's gonna drown soon, so I go down and drag him up on the bank. "Get away, you smell bad....ohh...bad, bad smell..oh bad smell, Mommy," Willy mumbles, and then he mutters more words that I can't make out, just like when he talks in his sleep. Willy starts shaking all over, and he rubs his chest and his arms frantically. He tries to jump in the water again, but I grabs him and hauls him off to the tent.

When we got there, Willy was still shaking and pawing himself, and trying to run back to the stream. I just couldn't handle him, so I put his hands behind his back and tied him to a tree. Seeing that we had some warm water in the big pan on the stove, I poured some over Willy's head, but that didn't seem to help much. Willy was still shaking and mumbling things like, "bad smell....bad, Mommy," Poor Willy, I figured something real disgusting must have happened to him when he was a little kid, and somehow having that mammoth crap his half-cooked insides out all over us had reminded Willy of it so much he had slipped off his rocker and fallen back to being a little boy again.

I spent all night and all the next day heating water and washing up Willy and me and our clothes. I sure wished then that we each had an extra set of things to wear, and it would have helped too if we'd had any soap. I thought we both smelled pretty good after a couple of days, but I'd still get a nasty whiff if I sniffed at my shirt too close. Willy kept on with his babbling, and he wouldn't eat by himself. I tied him on his back to his bunk and forced some good moose broth soup down him without him upchucking more than part of it.

Things was pretty desperate, so I figured Willy and me had to get out of there. I packed up our gold and we took off downstream, me leading Willy with a rope so's to keep him out of the water and headed in the right direction. Two days later, we come to the Yukon just as a riverboat passing down from Dawson was going by. I waved, and the boat came over to pick us up.

"Jesus, you guys smell bad," the deck hand said as we came up the gangplank, and the captain wouldn't let us go inside the cabins. He even made us eat out on the deck instead of inside with the other passengers.

It's a good thing one of the passengers was a doctor. He gave Willy some pills to quiet him down and keep him from wanting to wash his hands all the time. The doctor also agreed—for a pretty high price—to take Willy out to Seattle with him and deliver him to Willy's brother, who lives with his family not far from there. I got off the boat at Ruby, mailed some gold and a letter to Willy's brother, and I spent the winter there.

Next summer, when I get back up the Tazitna River, to the place everybody now calls Elephant Gulch, I find things in pretty good shape. My new partner Oscar is with me, and we don't even notice much bad smell. Over the winter, the foxes and wolves has cleaned up the gulch real good. What they didn't eat, the ravens did. Oscar and me cleaned out the bones, put in a sluice box and did some serious mining. The paystreak didn't pinch out like I thought it might, so we've done real well ever since.

As we cleaned more of the muck away we found the mammoth's skull propped up in the air on the two big curving tusks that were jammed in against the rock walls of the gulch. We could have pried the thing down, but since we could walk underneath it, I left it hanging up there in Willy's memory. Poor Willy. He is not doing good, even yet. His brother writes to me that Willy is in a sanitarium where he lives in a spotless white room, wears a white gown and washes himself continuously.

I send money every year to pay for Willy's keep, he having been such a good partner to me. Oscar's OK, though. He works hard and he don't talk too much, but he can't read or write. He's awful sloppy and uncouth around camp, so I prefer to wash all the dishes myself. He wouldn't even wash his clothes proper if I didn't insist, and I make him do that every week. He also thinks it's funny to pass gas when we're in the tent together. I get perturbed 'cause every time Oscar does it my nostrils start twitching, and for an instant or two I live again the awful moment of Willy's undoing.

☀   ☀   ☀

The Ogilvie Gold Fibulator

The crowd was boisterous and entirely unappreciative of my first performance in the Climax Theatre. It was the worst audience I had faced in the two years since my graduation from the Philadelphia School of Drama and Oratory. As I headed off behind the curtain, the manager was in the wings, standing with his hands on his ample hips, and his eyes glowering belligerently beneath his green eyeshade. He reached over to swat the posterior of the scantily clad lady strutting past, on her way out to perform before the house. Catching sight of her, the uncouth louts now began cheering.

"What the hell do you think you're doing, mister, going out there before my crowd and spouting that Shakespeare crap?" the manager almost shouted. "I thought you were supposed to be a comic."

"I did understand that you preferred something light," I replied with dignity. "That is why my repertoire was from *A Midsummer Night's Dream* rather than *Hamlet,* which is my forte."

"You dumb sonofabitch, you're fired."

"Sir," I said, drawing myself up and squaring my shoulders, "may I remind you that we have a contract. I have a copy of it as executed by my agent in Boston. It says..."

"Screw your agent in Boston, buddy. Here's three bucks. Now get your ass out of here."

I dare say that I was highly insulted. My face burned as I picked up my valise from the dressing room and headed out past the old doorman who sat hunched over a pulp magazine on his desk, eating a sandwich. He belched loudly as I swung the door open and entered the alley. The passageway also was disgusting; I had to tread carefully to avoid the ripe garbage spilling out beside the back doorway of the restaurant next door. Oh why had I come to San Francisco? Of course I knew why: it was the only booking I could get, and that added to my despair.

I was still despondent as I sat in a nearby establishment finishing my first libation, and quite in the mood to order another, when a most respectable-looking older gentleman sat down beside me. "Good evening, son," he said with a kindly smile, "For someone so elegantly dressed, you seem to be feeling a bit low."

Low indeed, I was in possession of my valise and $2.75, with no prospect for the future whatsoever, and not even a room for the night because I had arrived on the train with barely enough time to make my initial—alas, my last—performance in the Climax.

"Ah, an actor you say, that's interesting...." the kindly old gentleman mused, after I had explained my situation. Then I saw him glance over my shoulder toward the entryway. "Be right back," he said briskly, sliding off his stool in the direction of the men's lavatory. Shortly afterwards, two of the local gendarmerie sauntered past with eyes roving over the crowd in the smoky room.

The man soon returned, and we continued our conversation over several additional drinks. As the evening progressed, I felt increasing kindly toward Mr. Ogilvie—Mr. Samuel Ogilvie, he said during our introductions. From the words he used and his manner of speech, I could tell he was a cultured and learned man. He also was so genuinely interested in my welfare that, before the evening was over, he suggested that I become his travelling companion.

"You can call me Samuel, Joseph, and you need not be concerned with your present shortage of funds. Your situation will soon improve, and you will have opportunity to make good use of your skills. Now please join me in my hotel suite for the remainder of the evening. It contains more than adequate room for us both. We will get a good night's sleep, then tomorrow we journey on."

I was so overcome with my sudden good turn of fortune—and perhaps also affected by the consumption of several drinks purchased by Mr. Ogilvie—that I failed that evening to understand the exact nature of what he had in mind for me, or to where my travels with him might lead. Oh well, as spoke The Bard, "All in good time."

Over a delightful breakfast brought to Mr. Ogilvie's rooms, we continued our discussion, and from part of it I gathered that Samuel was perhaps not as wealthy as he appeared. With an oblique remark or two, Samuel ascertained that I was not unfamiliar with whist and other cards, so I suspected that he might be a professional gambler. Still confused about his occupation, if any, I put the question to him directly.

"Certainly not," he said emphatically, "although I must admit I do on occasion enjoy a rousing game of poker. Sometimes I am even lucky enough to win, and that of course makes the experience more pleasurable. Indeed, the proper application of a man's skill can provide a means to supplement his fiscal resources if the need arises. But a gambler, sir, that I am not." Samuel seemed indignant that I had brought up the issue.

He then said he had a few errands to run, and would return. Two hours later he was back bearing several small packages and two envelopes, one of which he presented to me. Inside was a ticket for passage, meals and a stateroom aboard the steamer *Cudahay* bound for Valdez, a destination unfamiliar to me, but one obviously named after the famous Spanish explorer whom I had studied in prep school. I presumed that it must be somewhere down the California coast or even farther, and I conjured up an image of red-roofed stucco mansions overlooking a palm-studded sandy beach and maidens splashing in the warm blue waters beyond. How fortunate I was to have chanced across Samuel Ogilvie.

Then Mr. Ogilvie engaged me in further conversation, the turn of which surprised me. It seemed that after the purchase of our passage toward a warmer clime, Mr. Ogilvie was, as he stated, somewhat embarrassed by a temporary shortage of funds. The hotel manager had generously permitted Mr. Ogilvie to engage his suite without advance payment in view of the expected arrival of a bank draft "from my home office," payable to the manager so that he could subtract monies due and turn over the remainder to Samuel.

The bank draft had not yet arrived, explained Mr. Ogilvie, "...and in view of our need to embark this afternoon, I might suggest to the manager that he retain our bill until the draft arrives, then forward the balance on to us at Valdez. However, knowing hotel managers as I do, I am not sure that he would be agreeable. Joseph, my boy, we are about to embark upon the first real-life test of your thespian abilities. Now let us retire to the dining room for one last grand repast in this establishment."

"Good day, Mr. Pearson...ah, I see you have a guest today."

"Yes, thank you, James, a table here by the door please," Mr. Ogilvie responded.

After we were seated, I commented, "For a head waiter, he seems to have a rather poor memory. He called you Mr. Pearson."

"No, Joseph, he has a fine memory," replied Samuel.

While I pondered the implication of this remark, another waiter came up, and Samuel ordered a not inexpensive meal for us both. Presently, he outlined to me the activities he proposed we undertake during the next few hours.

"But, Samuel, that is illegal—in the East it is called defrauding an innkeeper. I cannot go along with such a plan."

"Indeed, the same term applies here, but this innkeeper is one of the despicable kind who overcharges, and the circumstances require special action. Do you choose to join me aboard the *Cudahay* two hours hence, or do you prefer to spend the next few nights in the local stockade? It is a most unpleasant place, I am informed, and I understand that handsome young men like yourself do not fare well there, even for one night."

Samuel's argument was persuasive. Best to go along, I rationalized, though in retrospect perhaps I had other options.

Almost finishing his meal, Samuel left, and a few minutes later I carefully watched the dial over the elevator door detail that conveyance's progress toward the lobby from its initial position on the floor of Samuel's suite. At the appropriate moment, just as the elevator door was about to open, I choked loudly, jumped up from the table in fair semblance of having an epileptic fit that bowled over my table with a loud crash and carried me out the restaurant doorway, my arms flailing and my whole body quivering. The horrified expressions on the faces of all onlookers as their eyes followed me to my final collapse behind the front lobby desk testified to the realism of my performance.

Several minutes later, long after Samuel had escaped out the front door bearing his packages, his suitcase and my valise, I recovered enough to request that the bellhop and the doorman help me outside for some fresh air. They and the manager, all who had given me their undivided attention almost from the start, were happy to comply. There, I thanked them profusely and asked that they let me sit in silence for a few minutes before retiring to Mr. Pearson's suite.

Other matters soon occupied them, and within the hour I was handing my ticket to the *Cudahay's* purser, with the explanation that my baggage would soon arrive. When the steward brought me to my cabin, I found my valise already inside and a nearby envelope addressed to me. The note inside read, "Well done, Joseph, a most convincing performance. I knew I had picked the right man. Best remain in your cabin until after we sail, and remember, you do not know me. When the time is right I will introduce myself. Follow my lead, and we go on from there.—S. O.

"P.S. I have ordered a bottle of champagne for your cabin. Bon Voyage, My Friend!" And so that is how I became associated with Samuel Ogilvie. That, I assumed, was his true name, for he used it comfortably.

Sitting there in my cabin, I came close to tears of remorse. I, who had never had the slightest dishonest inclination in my life, that day had committed a terrible crime. I popped the cork of the champagne bottle, and as I slowly sipped I resolved to prepare a letter of apology to the hotel manager and at the first opportunity send it to him with a promise to repay whatever amount Samuel owed. Then as I sipped further, it occurred to me that perhaps I had not actually committed a crime at all—I had merely put on one of the better performances of my acting career. Really, I had done nothing wrong at all. Soon, my intent to write a letter dissolved in the better part of the bottle of bubbly. In the meantime, the ship had departed the wharf and was steaming out through the Golden Gate. I went out on deck to enjoy the view.

Taking note of the other passengers for the first time, I saw them to be primarily a raffish lot, and most were roughly dressed for such a cruise. Then as we cleared the strait, I was surprised to feel the ship wheeling to the right. Must be to avoid an incoming vessel, I conjectured, until a nearby passenger joyfully said to his companion, "We did it, George, now we're truly headed for Alaska."

Alaska! My mind reeled. Oh no, this can't be. Had I boarded the wrong ship? No, before me on the rail hung a life preserver labeled "S.S. Cudahay." I ran to a crossways where I had seen a map of the Pacific Coast when boarding, and as I inspected the map, the awful truth dawned: Valdez *was* in Alaska. Samuel Ogilvie, the scoundrel, could have at least told me where we were going. I might not have chosen to travel on with him, I decided, as I headed back to the cabin to finish my champagne.

I nodded off and slept so soundly I failed to awake for supper. I was ravenous when I rose the next morning, and so was among the first to enter the dining area. Eventually Samuel arrived, taking no note of me as he walked past my seat and settled himself at the opposite end of the other long table in the room. Although I could not hear his words, I saw that he was introducing himself to those nearby, and I observed that he maintained animated conversation with them during the remainder of the meal.

And so it went as the *S.S. Cudahay* steamed up the coast past Seattle and entered the Inside Passage. I spent my time in my cabin, walking the deck and partaking of meals. I saw Samuel on deck numerous times and also during the meals. He was always talking with someone—he seemed to have become acquainted with everyone aboard—but he never talked with me.

Then after supper on the third night out, Samuel knocked briefly and slipped into my cabin. "Joseph, my boy," he said, "the time has come to replenish our finances. We will need a little spending money as we proceed on to the gold fields from Valdez. Here is the plan: I have selected a few men who are adequately endowed with funds, plus a passenger who obviously is a shark. Here's what you are to do...."

Samuel was already seated with four others around one of the tables in the salon when I entered late that evening. As instructed by Samuel, I walked up to the bar to order. In the process I displayed a large roll of bills, which in fact consisted of only one large bill wrapped around a small one and a number of sheets of worthless paper prepared by Samuel. "Now don't lose it," he had admonished. "Except for this one other bill, that's all I've got."

As I began to sip my drink, Samuel called out, "Hello, young feller, care to join us in a friendly game?" He winked knowingly to one of his companions, and continued, "We could make room for him, couldn't we, gentlemen?"

"Of course," rejoined the man, pulling up another chair for me. He, I presumed, was the card shark.

"Well, I just came in for a nightcap. I sometimes play cards, but it appears that you are playing poker, and I know little of the game. Perhaps I might just sit down and watch."

I waited until it was the shark's turn to deal, then said that I might join the game after all. "It does look like good sport," I said, "I might try a hand or two." As Samuel had predicted, I won that first hand—and with only two pairs, and that was fortunate because I had bet nearly all the money Samuel had given me. But now, I had a stake.

I displayed increasing enthusiasm for the game as the evening progressed. For good reason, too, because nearly each time the shark dealt, I won, and several times also when Samuel handled the deck. He also won, but far more modestly. Finally, when I saw I was ahead by nearly two hundred dollars, I yawned deeply and said. "Gentlemen, I must retire. This has been an enjoyable evening, but I am simply worn out."

"Well, sir," said Samuel, "we've enjoyed your

company, even if you did relieve us of some of our funds. We will be playing again tomorrow night. Why don't you join us again?"

"Oh I think not...well...perhaps. I will think about it. Good night, gentlemen."

Samuel entered my cabin a little later, smiling broadly. "I've got him hooked," Samuel said with glee. "He doesn't suspect a thing. I put the bite on him by telling him that I knew he was a card cheat and that I had half a mind to turn him in to the captain. Then I took pity and got him to agree to give me thirty percent of the take if I could get you back into the game tomorrow so he could clean you out with my help. I told him you probably had about $5000 in that roll, and with any luck at all he and I could get a fair portion of it. Now tomorrow night, make sure you sit to my immediate right, and I'll be on his right. I figure he'll be willing to let you get ahead by about a thousand before he's ready to deal you the sucker hand. But by then he's apt to get a little too greedy, and I'll be one chair in front of him. I'll give you the sign just when he's ready for it." Samuel pulled out a deck of cards, and I practiced making a few cuts for him.

Everything went as Samuel predicted. This was the last night out, so the ship was rolling in the rough waters of the Gulf of Alaska, even more than Samuel had suggested it might. Despite the growing pile of bills in front of me, I was showing signs of suffering from the motion—and it was not entirely all acting, I fear. When Samuel decided we had gone as far as possible, and it was his turn to deal, he kicked me under the table. I cut the cards for him as instructed, and prepared myself. My appearance of queasiness increased as Samuel took $50 from me that hand and over $500 from the sharpster. The man's eyes squinted suspiciously, but it was too late for him.

Clutching my winnings in one hand as I staggered to my feet, I leaned over the table and erupted a guttural gurgling sound that growled up from my stomach and passed out between my lips along with a previously stored cheekful of water—all over the unfortunate gambler. "Oohh, Argh, I'm sick," I moaned, rushing out the salon door to lean over the rail and continue my gagging noises.

Behind me, I could hear Samuel consoling the card sharp, "Oh God, he got it all over you. I'll get him into his cabin while you clean yourself up. We'll do better next time, friend."

The following morning as Samuel and I left the *Cudahay* in Valdez harbor we were nearly $2000 richer than when we boarded. The gambler, who we knew was returning to San Francisco, stood at the head of the gangplank watching. "You sons-of-bitches," he said, his face angry.

"Now, now, my good fellow," replied Samuel, "A professional man always retains his composure. Give my regards to the captain."

As we walked onto the wharf I said to Samuel, "I feel bad about what we did. Sure, he is card sharp, but nevertheless..."

"Forget it, Joseph. With all these people waiting to join him on his return trip, he will be twice as rich as we are by the time he gets to San Francisco. Besides, I have no sympathy for a man who earns his living in such an underhanded fashion."

Valdez was even worse than I feared. Admittedly, the surrounding mountains were spectacular, and I had never seen glaciers before, but the town itself was a rude collection of wooden buildings surrounded by hastily erected tents. Men, all wearing mud-covered boots, were milling around everywhere. The center of activity was on the wharf, which was rapidly disappearing under mounds of boxes and other freight coming off the *Cudahay*.

I sensed a new mystery surrounding Samuel Ogilvie as I spied two men wheeling a large crate down the ramp. Painted boldly across one side were the words "Professor Samuel Ogilvie," and beneath that was a temporary placard reading "Valdez via S.S. Cudahay."

"What's the deal, Samuel?" I queried. "Professor? And what's in the box?"

"Yes, Professor Samuel P. Ogilvie, recently on the faculty of Oxnard Technological College. From now on in the presence of others, Joseph, you shall call me 'Professor.' The box? Oh, just a few miscellaneous possessions." Already, I had learned enough about Samuel to know that further questioning was useless.

We took a room in what passed for a hotel. That night and the next I slept in the last comfortable bed I would see for many days, for we were soon on the stage bound for the Tanana gold camps, some three hundred miles distant. The discomfort I endured during that hazardous journey through endless swamp-filled valleys and across rugged mountain passes is beyond my ability to describe. Samuel, excuse me, the Professor, seemed to enjoy the trip. As we bounced along with his large crate lashed to the rear of the stage, he chatted happily with other passengers and kept an interested eye on our surroundings. I endured the days and hated the nights, since each evening the stage stopped at a vile-smelling way station called a "roadhouse." There, we dined on badly cooked fare evidently derived from the various horned ruminants that populated the local countryside, and which we on occasion saw from the stage. We then slept in the very same room, sometimes three together on pole benches without any mattresses whatsoever.

At that, I felt somewhat lucky, for most of the people in transit to the gold fields were actually walking the entire distance. Many of the poor wretches carried heavy loads on their shoulders or pushed and pulled carts loaded with their belongings. Thank God for the gambler, I thought; were it not for him, I probably would be out on that horrible track beneath Samuel's crate.

We eventually arrived in the main gold camp of the area, Fairbanks, a town equally as crude as Valdez, but much larger. I was surprised at the number of saloons and other business establishments and about how many people they were serving until I learned that the area had several other large encampments nearby, all within an easy day's travel. Samuel found us lodging in a rooming house near the center of the town, not far from the river where several paddle-wheelers were discharging freight.

While I wandered around to get more familiar with the place, Samuel went off "on an errand," and I wondered what its consequences held for me. On his return he handed me a sack containing a new hammer and a few nails while saying, "Joseph, the time has come to begin some serious work."

Oh Lord, I thought, what now? I hefted the hammer gingerly, it being a device to which I was thoroughly unaccustomed. Samuel then led me down the street and over a short block to an empty one-room cabin built of logs. Propped against the front wall next to the doorway stood Samuel's large crate. "This will be our base of operations," he said. "Now let's get this box open."

Soon recognizing my ineptness, Samuel impatiently grabbed the hammer, and with it pried and pounded away the two longest walls of the crate, exposing inside only an assortment of smaller boxes of various sizes. My curiosity shifted to the meaning of the identical lettering painted on the inside faces of the two crate walls:

**AMALGAMATED METALS
EXPLORATION, Ltd.**

FAIRBANKS FIELD OFFICE
Prof. Samuel P. Ogilvie, Director

I was stunned, for everything I had seen of Samuel so far implied to me that his every action was on the spur of the moment. That was not so; obviously we had come to Fairbanks for a purpose, but one still unknown to me. In awed silence I held the crate sides while Samuel nailed them together at one end, and then we placed the triangular assembly up above the cabin door to form a sign easily visible from either approach along the street. We then carried into the cabin the crate's inner boxes, some with difficulty, for they were extremely heavy.

"Thanks, Joseph; you run along now and enjoy the town while I take care of things here. If anyone asks what you are doing in town, just tell them you work for me."

"So what will I be doing, Professor, honest work?"

"Well, nothing illegal, certainly, but I assure you that it will be highly remunerative. I'll see you later, Joseph."

I walked away thinking that I might be wise to sever my relationship with Samuel Ogilvie. But then what would I do in this godforsaken place? The answer leapt out from a poster announcing the arrival of a performing group from Seattle two days hence. That's it, I thought. I was, after all, an actor, so perhaps I could obtain a position with that troupe or some other.

Over supper that evening I voiced my thoughts to Samuel. He remained silent for a few moments, and then surprised me with his response, "I quite understand, Joseph. I would hate to see you drop our association. But do what you think best. You are an excellent actor with a bright future ahead. Think it over for a few days, and if you still choose to leave, I will hand you a share of our earnings to date. Now, I have some business to attend to in the morning, but I have hired a buggy for the afternoon, and I suggest you come with me to view some of the gold fields. You will find it interesting."

The afternoon was interesting, in an odd sort of way. We travelled westerly through swampy countryside to a place Samuel said was called Berry or Ester, here and there along the way seeing men working in and around excavations. We stopped once near the base of a long slope, up on which we could see a vast number of small pits, each with one or two men busy at enlarging them.

"They look like a bunch of gophers, don't they?" chuckled Samuel. "Most of those damn fools are digging at random. They have absolutely no idea of where gold should lie."

All that we saw that afternoon increased my resolve to continue my acting career. I certainly did not choose to become involved in mining in any form whatsoever, and it appeared that if I stayed with Samuel Ogilvie such an involvement was highly likely—if he was who he claimed to be. I would pursue the matter of a new job as soon as the acting troupe arrived.

When our buggy again approached the town, we saw a large sternwheeler churning up the nearby river. Samuel jogged the reins, and our pace increased until we came abreast of the boat on a turn of the river. "Aha, it's the *Yukon,*" he exclaimed, "Perfect timing." Samuel continued to hurry the horse along, and we were waiting by the bank when the boat docked. I scanned my eyes over the passengers waiting to disembark until they came to rest on a vision. Just then, the vision waved and called out in a loud but lovely voice, "Professor, I'm here."

"Who's that?" I said, my eyes wide.

"That, Joseph, is Priscilla, my most able office manager. You will meet her shortly."

My eyes never left her as she tripped daintily across the gangplank, her full skirt brushing between the narrow stanchions, and came toward us. "Oh, I'm so happy to see you," she trilled and reached out to embrace Samuel Ogilvie and receive from him a peck on the cheek. Samuel then took her by the arm and introduced me.

"Priscilla, my dear, this is Joseph Buckley, a talented young man I met in San Francisco and who has been travelling with me. I had rather hoped that he might join our firm, but I understand that he has other plans." Then to me he said, "Joseph, if you would be so kind as to remain here to collect Miss Osborne's baggage, I will show her to the Pioneer Hotel, where I also have taken up a room. Perhaps you will join us for supper there later."

They went off arm in arm chatting happily, and so I stayed by the dock wondering if Priscilla Osborne might be more to Samuel Ogilvie than merely his office manager. My first impression was that she seemed fond of him, and he of her. It was a discouraging thought, for I found her extremely attractive. I sensed an inner charm as well, something quite beyond what I had noticed in any woman before.

I was even more enamored with Priscilla by the end of the evening, an evening spent over a good meal and involving several entertaining stories by Priscilla as she told about her journey to visit an aunt in Pocatello, then onward via Seattle and St. Michael, where she had boarded the *Yukon* for the trip upriver to Fairbanks. During the course of the meal I was somewhat relieved to observe that Samuel's Ogilvie's attitude toward her was entirely proper, as was hers toward him. She always referred to him as "Professor" and I loved the lilt in her voice when she said it. I felt even better later when Samuel requested that I remain at the table for further conversation. "I will escort Miss Osborne to her room and promptly return," he said. In fact, he was soon back.

"All is going well, Joseph. Now that Miss Osborne has arrived, I will be ready to open my office tomorrow and get down to work. I am sorry that you will be going your own way because your services would be invaluable to me. I had hoped that you would participate in the effort with me and my lovely assistant. But of course I understand your desires to further your own career, and I realize that having to work in close association with a lady is awkward, especially a young unmarried one like Priscilla, for then a man must always be on his best behavior. That can be most wearing, and I can see that you might prefer not to put up with it."

"Well, er, well, Professor," I stammered, my face reddening slightly, "I've been thinking it over, and perhaps I might reconsider."

"Yes, I thought you might," he replied rather dryly, and my face reddened even more. But then he continued, "I'm delighted, Joseph. I must inform you that Miss Osborne works on commission, and I am prepared to make the same arrangement with you. Like her, you shall receive ten percent of net proceeds, and I guarantee that your earnings will far exceed that of any actor you know. Enough for to-night, Joseph. Be at the office in the morning and I will fill you in on the details." He then retired to his room. Having cast aside my doubts about Professor Ogilvie, I sauntered to my rooming house full of anticipation with the morrow.

Professor Ogilvie and Priscilla were already there when I arrived at the office. The professor was busy unpacking boxes and Priscilla was arranging papers and other office materials on a desk and bookcase that had somehow miraculously appeared. I was torn between observing her and watching the professor as he extracted from the boxes one wondrous item after another and laid it out on a bench or on the floor. Before me was a growing assemblage of mysterious metal objects, wires and a large finely finished wooden cabinet from which levers and dials projected.

"What is all this stuff, Professor?" I queried, and this time I got an answer.

"This, my boy, is my finest invention, the Ogilvie Gold Fibulator."

"What does it do?"

"It makes gold mining profitable. Joseph, the problem with gold is that it is dispersed in massive amounts of soil and rock, within deposits difficult to find and excavate. The Fibulator is used both to locate wealth and concentrate it," said Samuel as he carefully inspected an intricate component to ascertain its freedom from shipping damage, "Ah, yes, perfect," he continued.

"Level with me, Professor, does this thing really work?"

"Listen to our skeptical young friend, Miss Osborne," Samuel exclaimed. Priscilla smiled sweetly and reassuringly at me as the Professor continued, "It certainly does, and with it I intend to increase the profits of many miners in the area, while also receiving adequate compensation for myself and my associates." Priscilla continued on with her duties, which now consisted of unpacking a box of books and loading them on the bookcase. I noticed that these books all had complex scientific titles. They had been properly cared for but appeared well used. I also noticed that as Miss Osborne lifted up the books, she displayed a lovely profile.

Meanwhile I gave minor assistance to Samuel as he assembled his equipment, of which I could make sense of only one part. That was a miniature steam engine, little more than three feet long. It was beautifully machined, painted red and gray, and it had

shiny brass fittings. This engine, it appeared, powered the Fibulator, for the Professor soon had it attached by a smooth endless belt to the cabinet which
contained the levers and dials, plus an incredibly
complicated array of internal workings. I was awed
by the dexterity and knowledge the Professor displayed as he went about his work, however not so
awed that I failed to continue to observe Priscilla
pursue her tasks, displaying both efficiency and
charm.

When all was done, Samuel stood back with a
self-satisfied look, and then said, "We are ready for
the next step. Joseph, you now will learn what you
are to do. As you know, Priscilla—Miss Osborne,
that is—will manage our office and keep our ac-
counts. She will also on occasion accompany us to
the gold fields as note-taker during the operation of
the Ogilvie Gold Fibulator. On these excursions and
elsewhere when we are in public we shall maintain
an air of formality. Notice that Miss Osborne, as is
fitting, always refers to me as "Professor," and you
shall continue to do the same. Likewise, I will call
you both by your proper names when we are in the
presence of others. Also, Joseph, to avoid future er-
ror, best you refer to me as "Professor," even in pri-
vate. Now, my boy, your tasks will be several. The
only one involving physical labor will be the job of
maintaining a fuel supply for the engine that drives
the Fibulator and inserting that fuel in the firebox as
the need arises. You will assist me in its operation
because that requires two people. I will be the opera-
tor, and you will, in a sense, become part of the ma-

chine."

"Part of the machine?"

"Yes, Joseph, the Fibulator operates jointly on the principles of electrophorosis and electrophysicosism. Thus it requires the presence of a human being in the circuitry. Not just any human being, mind you, but one of sensitive nature like yourself."

"I don't follow you," I replied, trying to make sense of what he was saying.

"You will see shortly. Now help me drag the steam engine and the Fibulator out the rear door of the cabin, so we can build a fire in the boiler."

Thirty minutes later, enough steam had been produced to begin turning the steam engine. I watched with interest as it began to drive the Fibulator, which in itself seemed to do nothing. Then the professor opened another box and took out a mysterious object.

"Looks sort of like a helmet, but it's got two rods sticking up out of the top of it," I observed.

"Right you are, Joseph, that's the Fibulation Helmet. It goes on your head, and these two leads hook onto your ears. Are you ready?"

"I don't know," I said, "What's it going to do to me? Will it hurt?"

"No, no, my boy, you won't feel a thing, except for a tingling in your ears from time to time when we get exact electroosmotic tuning during Stage One Fibulation. Miss Osborne, will you assist Mr. Buckley into the Fibulation Helmet?"

My trepidation melted away as Priscilla approached me, and smiled sweetly as she placed the strange helmet on my head and attached the leads to my earlobes. I savored her perfume as she then reached around me and placed on my waist a wide black leather belt from which a heavy wire ran up to the Fibulation Helmet. Priscilla backed away, and the Professor reached toward the Fibulator. He withdrew from it the end of a covered wire which he plugged into the wires attached to the rear of the belt.

"Now, Priscilla, hand him the Fibulation Bar and plug it into the Fibulation Belt," he said, and she reached into a long, narrow box to remove a strange metal bar, some six feet long and sharply pointed on one end. Its other bore a glass ball about the size of a man's head. Midway along the bar and several feet apart were two small protruding wooden loops.

"Grasp it by the handles, Joseph," the Professor said, as Priscilla handed me the bar and then attached a wire trailing out from it to a socket on the Fibulation Belt. "Now hold it out horizontally at arm's length and just let your mind go blank," instructed the Professor. "Let your face relax, and look straight ahead, and when you hear a buzzing sound in the Fibulation Helmet start walking. You may sense that the Fibulation Bar is trying to pull you along, although the sensation may be so slight as to be subconscious. Then when your left ear tingles, turn left, and when the right ear tingles, turn right. When both ears tingle, lean over and touch the end of the Fibulation Bar to the floor. When all that happens we will have achieved complete Stage 1 Fibulation. In short, the Fibulator has guided you to the highest concentration of gold in the area. Let's give it a try."

Feeling somewhat foolish standing there before Priscilla like that, I let my face relax with my eyes focused straight ahead and tried to let my mind go blank, as instructed. Professor Ogilvie sat down in front of the Fibulator box and began turning dials.

"Getting any buzzing yet?" he queried.

"No, but I can't make my mind go blank."

"Try thinking about something pleasant," he said, so I thought about Priscilla.

I heard the buzzing noise. "I got it," I said.

"Good, good; now start walking."

I could not be sure, but I did seem to sense some tugging sensation from the Fibulation Bar. Soon my right ear tingled, so I turned right. "Keep it up, Joseph, we're getting perfect fibulation," said the professor, and then my left ear tingled, so I turned that way. The Fibulator guided me around the room until the professor threw a switch and said, "That's enough, Joseph."

"I never did get a tingling in both ears, though," I said, laying down the Fibulation Bar and taking off the Fibulation Helmet.

"No, of course not," said Professor Ogilvie. "That is because there is no gold here, but it's working perfectly. We're about ready to put the Fibulator into the field. Shortly thereafter, money should be coming our way. Now run along, Joseph. You can take the rest of the day off; Priscilla—Miss Osborne—and I have other work to do."

The next day, both Priscilla and I accompanied

Professor Ogilvie out to Ester, she having brought along a picnic basket. I did not mind at all that the Professor left me alone with Priscilla most of the morning as he wandered around the various diggings in the area and talked with some of the miners. I enjoyed being alone with her for the first time, but I fear that I did most of the talking, and she seemed to enjoy a few of my recitations from Shakespeare. Eventually the Professor returned; we three had a most delightful lunch, and then he suggested that Priscilla and I walk with him.

With Priscilla and me trailing behind, the Professor strode purposefully past several of the diggings. The various miners about took great interest in our progress, and I found that I was bothered by seeing their eyes follow Priscilla so closely as she tripped serenely along beside me. Eventually we approached the Professor's objective, one of the larger of the workings where several men were busy beside a long sluice box. The Professor walked up to the man I took to be their supervisor.

"Mr. Swanson, I have returned, and now I have a business proposition for you. I wish to bring my invention, the Ogilvie Gold Fibulator, onto your property to see if your gold-bearing deposit is amenable to location and concentration with my device. If so, your profits may soon increase."

"Well, I don't know," replied Mr. Swanson. "We're doing pretty well here as it is."

"Yes, but I believe you can do better. Should you choose to allow this test with my equipment and if it fails to increase your next clean-up over the value of the last, then you owe me nothing. That might well happen because the Fibulator requires that the soil have certain electrophoretic properties, and that can not be known in advance. Now, however, if you agree to the test, and the Fibulator succeeds, my fee will be minor, merely twenty percent of the excess gold you recover on clean-up over the value of the one you last undertook prior to the Fibulation treatment."

Mr. Swanson thought for a while and then said, "See no harm in giving it a chance, I guess. Seems like I have nothing to lose."

"Precisely, sir. We will return with the Ogilvie Gold Fibulator in a day or so. Miss Osborne, an agreement form please." Priscilla removed a sheet of paper from her bag. The Professor read aloud a short paragraph detailing the arrangement, then signed with a flourish and handed the paper to Mr. Swanson. He examined it carefully, then too signed with a laborious hand.

The Professor led us on to two other diggings where he and the responsible miners concluded similar agreements. "Well, Miss Osborne and Mr. Buckley, we are in business," the Professor said as we climbed back onto our buggy and he signaled with the reins for the horse to proceed.

As we drove back to Fairbanks, I thought over what I had heard, and I was particularly puzzled by one thing. "Professor," I asked, "how will you know whether the miners will pay you for the use of the Fibulator? I mean, even if it increases the gold they get, they could just claim that they are getting no more gold than before. What's to stop them from that?"

"Don't be concerned, Mr. Buckley. Miners are hard-working, honest men. If the Fibulator increases their earnings, they will share the wealth with us. Have no fear; honest men never cheat, and of course you can never really cheat them. Always remember that, Mr. Buckley."

The next day we attracted quite a crowd as the Professor, Priscilla and I rode out to Mr. Swanson's diggings with the Fibulator mounted on the wagon behind us. Soon after we left town, the Professor had me start a fire in the boiler, and by the time we entered the mining area, excess steam was wheezing out the escape valve, leaving a white trail behind us. Many of the miners we passed dropped their tools and fell in with us. They all seemed to know why we were there and where we were headed, for by the time we arrived, other men were waiting beside Mr. Swanson's sluice box to see the Fibulator operate.

"We could use some help, here," the Professor said, and several men eagerly helped me lift the Fibulator and its engine off the wagon. "Bring it up here, fellows," commanded the Professor, striding off upstream to a place where Swanson's men had cleared away the moss and trees to make ready for future mining. "Careful, boys; now set it down right here."

I went back to the wagon to get the rest of the equipment, which included the Fibulation Helmet, the Fibulation Bar and the Fibulation Belt. I also brought over two folding chairs, one for Priscilla and one for the Professor.

"Check the fuel, Mr. Buckley; we are ready to begin," said the Professor, so I put two sticks of wood in the boiler and prepared to don the helmet and belt. The crowd of miners watched with great interest as Priscilla helped me into the paraphernalia. The Professor then sat down on a chair before the Fibulator and turned on the boiler valve. The steam engine began to puff away, "whoosh, whoosh, whoosh." Looks of awe and anticipation covered the faces of the watching miners, and several of them stepped backward as the steam engine began to turn.

"Gentlemen," the Professor said importantly to the assembled gathering, "first we have to tune the Fibulator to Mr. Buckley's special brain patterns. As you will soon see, he is a man of unique talents, for with the aid of the Fibulator he will be able to locate the main concentration of gold in the immediate area. Are you ready, Mr. Buckley?"

"Ready, Professor."

"Prepare for Fibulator tuning, Miss Osborne. Write down everything I say." Priscilla opened her notepad in readiness, looking intent, and very pretty, I thought. As the Professor began turning dials, he called out a series of numbers that Priscilla wrote down. I stood stock still, let my face go blank and stared straight ahead as I held the Fibulator Bar out before me. Soon I heard the buzzing noise, so began walking forward.

"Good, good, Miss Osborne. He is properly

tuned. We are proceeding with Stage One Fibulation."

"Jeez, look at that," a watching miner said with wonder. "He looks spooky, just like somebody put a hex on him."

Accompanied by the group of interested men, I slowly ambled forward, still holding the Fibulation bar horizontally and well out in front. Soon I felt a slight tingling in my right ear, so I let the Fibulator bar turn me slightly in that direction. A little later it came again, so I turned farther to the right and continued until a tingling in my left ear told me to turn that way and continue. The wire attaching me to the Fibulator reeled out of the machine as I walked along, turning now and again in response to the tingling in one ear or the other. In the meantime the Professor was calling out a steady stream of numbers, and Priscilla was writing them down. Only once did he interrupt himself to call out, "Don't get too close to him, boys; he's hot."

I had walked about a hundred feet, my tether trailing out behind me, when I felt a strong jolt in both ears, so strong that I nearly lost my senses. I staggered and almost fell over sideways as I jabbed the sharp end of the Fibulation Bar into the ground.

"He's found it, boys! Thirty-six ought four, Miss Osborne. Got that?"

"Yes, Professor."

Still feeling a little dazed, I removed the Fibulation Helmet and the Fibulation Belt, and then, as instructed by the Professor, placed the helmet on the rounded end of the Fibulation Bar and stepped back.

"Stage Two Fibulation; we're ready to attempt gold concentration. Everybody stand back!" called out Professor Ogilvie as he threw a large knife switch mounted on the front of the Fibulator.

I gasped, as did all the others except Priscilla and the Professor. He smiled broadly as a loud crackling noise erupted from the Fibulation Helmet, and what looked to be a bar of lightning rose up out of the helmet and slowly climbed up between the two protruding rods. I had never seen anything like that before, nor I imagine had anyone else other than my associates. All was silence for a few moments, then the crackling noise rang out again and another electrical arc climbed up the rods on the Fibulation Helmet.

"Wow!" "God almighty!" "Holy mackerel!" and other similar voicings of amazement sprang forth from the mouths of the watchers. The Fibulation Helmet erupted a few more cracklings and arcings before the professor again tripped the big knife switch on the front of the Fibulator, and it was over. When I got back near the Professor I whispered to him, "Damn it, Professor, that thing almost knocked me out. You told me it wouldn't hurt."

"Sorry about that, Joseph," he said in a low voice, "You seem to be even more sensitive than I thought. I guess I got the current set up a little too high. I'll ease off some next time."

The Professor then turned to Mr. Swanson saying, "Well, sir, I think we have done well for you. Notice that the Fibulator indicates that your richest ground is off to the right of where you are mining. I suggest that as you move up the stream you swing that direction some."

"You heard him, boys," Swanson said to his crew, "We'll give it a try over there." I could see that Mr. Swanson was impressed by our performance. The men standing around helped us load the Fibulator onto the wagon and accompanied us to the two other nearby mining properties on which the Professor had arranged for us to operate. We used the Fibulator at those locations as before. In each instance, before a watching crowd of miners, I plunged the Fibulation Bar into the ground at the places where the Fibulation Helmet gave me the signal, now sufficiently weakened that it caused only a brief twitching to course through my body.

Before the afternoon was over, several miners approached the Professor with requests to bring the Fibulator onto their properties. The Professor refrained from agreeing, but promised to visit those properties for initial examination. He told the men that the operation of the Fibulator took a lot out of me, and therefore that it was important to use the machine sparingly. The Professor said he would come and take soil samples to be analyzed in order to determine if the Fibulator was likely to operate successfully.

Very little happened during the following fortnight, other than that Professor Ogilvie went out almost every day in a buggy, returning each night with little bags of soil bearing labels such as "George Jorgeson, No. 4 Above Discovery, Eva Creek" or "Wilson Brothers, Jones Claim, Cripple Creek."

Priscilla took notes on each bag and placed them in a pile in the back of the office. As far as I could determine, no one ever touched them again. While the Professor was thus busy, Priscilla and I had almost no duties, so we spent our days walking about the town or going on picnics nearby. I recited readings and poetry to her, and told her my life story. She seemed to enjoy my company, but I sensed a certain reserve that somehow hid from me her true feelings.

Then one morning when the Professor and I arrived at the office of Amalgamated Metals Exploration, Ltd., a large crowd of miners was milling about and talking with Priscilla. "Well, Samuel," said the Professor, "I do believe that we have achieved a modicum of success. Let's see what all the excitement is about."

As we approached, a man stepped forward, wearing a large smile. I saw that it was Mr. Swanson, and that in his hand he carried a gold pouch. "Morning, Professor," he boomed out. "Got to hand it to you, that gadget of yours sure works. We cleaned up yesterday and got twice as much gold as before. Here's your twenty percent; there's pretty close to $2000 in this pouch. I'm mighty obliged to you, Professor, and if you'll bring that Fibulator thing back and show me where to mine next, I'd be real happy. I hear that Ed Murray was cleaning up too yesterday, and it looks like your Fibulator worked for him, too. Haven't heard about Lee Campbell's take. Guess he hasn't cleaned up yet."

Later in the day, Mr. Murray walked into the office, also smiling. He had not done quite so well on his cleanup as Mr. Swanson; still, our share of the increased take was nearly $1000. Lee Campbell reported in several days later, saying that his cleanup was slightly smaller than before.

"It is like I told you, Mr. Campbell," consoled the Professor, "Some of the mining ground hereabouts just doesn't have the right characteristics for exploration and concentration with the Fibulator. Unfortunately, yours seems to be of that type, although if you would like, I could try once more." Having of course heard about the other two successes, Mr. Campbell was eager to have us return.

"Not bad, you youngsters," chortled the Professor after Mr. Campbell was gone, "That's two out of three, and I suspect we are all on our way to getting rich."

I had to admit that up until then I was uncertain about the Fibulator. However, as they say, the proof is in the pudding: Mr. Swanson, Mr. Murray and the Professor, Priscilla and I were all richer than before. Furthermore, Mr. Campbell had lost nothing, and was even asking us to come back.

The next few weeks were horrible. A steady stream of miners besieged our office, all seeking to have the Professor bring the Fibulator to their properties. Poor Priscilla was almost beside herself trying to set up appointments for them to talk to the Professor. It was so bad that the Professor decided that Priscilla should remain in the office each day to deal with the horde and to keep up with an ever-increasing amount of record keeping and banking. "I think I can handle the note-taking myself," he explained, "and I think we best hire a strong young man to relieve Mr. Buckley of the task of boiler firing, and to help with the transportation of the Fibulator."

I was happy about that idea. Although I hated not having Priscilla accompany us out to the diggings, my boiler-firing and Fibulator-transporting duties were wearing me to a frazzle. We were going out on the average of two days out of three, usually managing to operate the Fibulator on at least two properties, and sometimes as many as four. Even the Professor was beginning to look a bit haggard, for on the days we did not operate the Fibulator he was out inspecting new properties and taking soil samples. The pile of soil bags in the back of the office was growing ever larger.

Day after day we were out on the creeks, our work threatening to become increasingly routine. At each chosen location, we fired up the boiler on the steam engine, the Professor fitted me into the Fibulation Belt and the Fibulation Helmet, and then I held out the Fibulation Bar and let all expression drain from my face. Then, as the Fibulation Helmet guided me by its tingling of my earlobes, I wandered around until the special signal told me to drive one end of the Fibulation Bar into the ground. Miners always congregated to watch my performances, and on some days even groups of women and children came out from the settlements to see the Fibulator in action.

Especially when the audience was large, I began adding little flourishes. Sometimes I executed what was almost a dance, placing one foot far out in front and then dragging the other along before stepping out again in an exaggerated manner. I performed slight twirling and bobbing motions with the Fibulation Bar, making it appear to have more of a life of its own than I could sense. Amidst "oohs" and "aahs" from the audience, I sometimes artfully staggered and nearly fell, but always recovered at the last moment. Then finally, when the Fibulation Helmet gave me the special signal I jammed the Fibulation Bar into the ground and used it as a fulcrum so that I could pick up my feet and click my heels before balancing again on my feet. These actions brought such cheers and applause from the crowd that I glowed inwardly at the end of each performance. This was better than being on stage, and definitely more remunerative.

"You're doing a damn fine job, Joseph; keep it up," the Professor whispered to me at the conclusion of one of my better shows.

Now that Elbert was helping us by keeping the boiler fired and doing general roustabout chores, I was truly beginning to enjoy the work, although for my taste we did far too much commuting on the hard seats of the wagon, and I did miss Priscilla's company on the trips. Best of all, however, was the money rolling in.

In truth, the Fibulator was successful but little over half the time. Nevertheless, our income was staggering, and the miners were happy with our work. After one clean-up alone, one over on Dome Creek, our share exceeded $10,000, and nearly $1000 of that was mine. By the end of the first six weeks we had taken in over $80,000, and the mining season had at least another month to go.

However, two things were bothering me greatly. One was Priscilla's continuing reserve toward me. I no longer could hide from myself that I was deeply in love with her, but I always sensed that a barrier remained between us, something that held her back from being completely open with me. The other thing bothering me was almost equally elusive.

One night when Priscilla, the Professor and I remained late at the office to tally up our take for that week, I stiffened my spine and came out with it.

"Professor, Priscilla, I've just got to talk. I've been thinking and pondering over what has been going on. We are making oodles of money and everybody seems satisfied, but I can't help but wonder if all this is right. It occurs to me, Professor, that your Fibulator might not do anything at all except make my ears tingle when you want them to tingle. The other thing that bothers me is why you go out on some days and collect all those soil samples. They just pile up here in the office, and you never do anything with them. Tell me, Professor, what the heck is going on? Are you being honest with me, with Priscilla, and with all these miners?"

Professor Ogilvie settled back in his chair, taking a long intent look at me. He then shifted his gaze to Priscilla, who cast her eyes downward and blushed.

"Well, my dear, this day is long overdue."

He turned back to me, saying, "Yes, my boy, I've been wondering when all this would come to the fore. Let me answer you by first posing a question. Let us just suppose that some man were to arrive in the gold fields with the assertion that he had the ability to wander over the surface of the ground and, merely by so doing, predict the most likely locations of the best gold deposits. Joseph, would the miners be likely to believe him?"

It was a rhetorical question, I recognized that right away.

Professor Ogilvie continued, "Now on the other hand, suppose that same man arrives on the creeks in somewhat different circumstances. His manner exudes knowledge and he is accompanied by a clean-cut young man who displays great respect for him, a most handsome and highly competent young lady who is equally respectful, and a scientific machine powered by a steam engine. Joseph, have you ever seen a man who failed to be impressed by another who appeared versed in scientific affairs and highly respected by his associates? Have you ever seen a man who failed to enjoy the sight of a pretty, unattached young lady, and who did not like to watch a well-constructed steam engine run? Or a man who was not intrigued with scientifically complex-looking machinery that might even help to make him rich? No, you have never met such a man. Think about all that, Joseph, and think about the tricks some of your fellow stage performers, the magicians, use to amaze their audiences. Put it all together, Joseph, and tell me what you conclude."

Even before he finished, I knew what the Professor was trying to tell me. I replied, "I guess I am a little disappointed. I was beginning to think that I really did have some special ability that the Fibulator brought out, but now I see that my participation is just for show. That Stage Two Fibulation is complete nonsense, isn't it? And the collection of the soil samples is merely a convincing excuse to walk around and inspect the mining properties. You are most deceitful, sir."

"Joseph, don't be such a skeptic. First off, let me assure you that you have far more ability than you suspect, and if you keep your eyes open as you grow older your ability will increase. But, more relevant to the issue you raise is the fact that most of the miners here have not the slightest idea where the best gold deposits are likely to occur. So I help guide their work by bringing to bear my observational powers and mental abilities."

"Are you really so skilled, Professor? Can you help them that much?"

"Indeed I can, Joseph. I am an experienced observer of both Mother Nature and human nature, and I have learned that what is useful in one arena often carries over to the other. Examine a man's face carefully, Joseph, for what you observe there in his eyes and the set of his mouth can tell you much about that man's past and his inner character. So it is with a stream valley. Each wrinkle on its weathered face has special meaning, for no dip or rise is ever accidental. It is always the result of some past interaction between resistive rocks and eroding waters. Streams—like human lives—rarely flow uniformly or from beginning to end in simple straight paths. They rage in spring and still in winter, and the courses they follow may be so complex as to appear accidental to the unobservant.

"But, my boy, nature does not have accidents. Everything that happens has an explainable cause. Observe carefully, Joseph, then think about the causes, and you may be able to detect where beneath each valley surface the gold should lie just as well as I."

"You are serious, Professor? You really can do it?"

"Certainly, Joseph. Were it not so, I assure you that we would not be pursuing this effort. When I walk onto a man's property—purportedly to take the soil samples—I look and ponder carefully. If what I see in the topography does not suggest that I may be able to help the miner, then we do not go back for the Fibulator show. Even so, I may not always be right; yet if I am right even only one time out of ten, it makes that miner richer."

"It makes us richer too, Professor. It occurs to me also that we get paid every time a miner's clean-up is better than the one before, and it seems like a fifty-fifty chance of that, even without the skills you claim."

"Ah yes, my boy, 'tis true. I've never believed in gambling."

"But, Professor, you told me once that it is impossible to cheat an honest man. These miners are honest men, but it seems to me that we steal from those of them who—totally by chance—get bigger cleanups after we've...well, fibulated them?"

"I note your humor, Joseph, and I like your honesty. Your question is a good one. However, my intentions are pure, so is there really a moral issue here? Why don't you discuss it with Priscilla? If you and she see it the same way, then I think you two may have a future together. Is that not correct, my dear?"

"Yes, Father," said Priscilla, blushing deeply and, for the first time, awarding me a completely open and loving smile.

❋　❋　❋

The Legacy of Double-Dose Dobson

For someone who was about to croak, old David Double-Dose Dobson was a surprisingly happy man. His twin offspring, Douglas and Donald, stood by his deathbed, each with tears rolling down his cheeks as Double-Dose said good-bye to me, and a last word to his sons: "It's all writ down proper in my will so's it's fifty-fifty, fair and square—she's all yours now, boys. Henry here helped me write it, and he's got the paper in the safe down at his store." He smiled one last smile, closed his eyes, and took the deep sleep. The reason Double-Dose was so happy was that he had always wanted to do well by his boys, and it had all worked out exactly the way he planned.

We started calling him Double-Dose because the old man had two of everything. He'd even had two wives. The first one died during the birth of Douglas and Donald; the second was a widow that Double-Dose hired to take care of the babies, and later married.

Double-Dose also owned two valleys, not big valleys, but both fairly productive of the gold that had
settled into their bottoms during the erosion of the
dome that the valleys flanked, side by side, on its
northern slope. Double-Dose staked the one little
valley himself, and after the boys were born he
bought out the claims a fellow miner had located in
the other.

I got to know Double-Dose pretty well, partly because he did most of his trading with me over the
years, even though the camp had other stores, and in
a way I was sort of an uncle to his boys. More than
most any man I ever knew, Double-Dose always put
great stock in fairness, especially when it came to his
two sons. He was proud as punch of those boys; I
thought maybe because they seemed to him like a
double image of himself. He was real broke up over
his first wife's death when they were born, so I suppose that also helps to explain why those boys were
so special to him. He wanted to do good by them,
and I figure that's why he bought the second valley
and got so engrossed with the idea of doing everything by twos. I realized later that Double-Dose really started going overboard on the whole business
when his second wife died, just six years after the
first. I was there the day we buried her beside the
grave of the other wife, exactly on the ridge top between Double-Dose's two valleys. I could tell he was
feeling particularly mortal that day, so the future of
the two boys was strongly in mind. Right away,
Double-Dose thought up a plan that he began to follow religiously.

I began to see what he was up to when Double-Dose started buying two of most everything, especially mining tools. Some of the other people in the camp thought he was acting strange, but I realized that Double-Dose knew what he was about.

Double-Dose's scheme could work because his two valleys were, like his boys, twins. "God has been good to me," Double-Dose said to me one day when he was feeling expansive, "He took my two wives away but He gave me two identical boys and two identical valleys with pay streaks just the same in width and depth, and the values per yard run just the same. I even got just the same ground yet to be mined. God made it equal, and I'm gonna do God's will for the boys."

As part of his plan to maintain the equality, Double-Dose took up the practice of mining in one valley on even-numbered years and in the other on odd years. Double-Dose was working the valleys from the bottom upward. At the rate he was going, he would be able to mine like that for decades. Since I'd helped him write his will, I knew the plan. If Double-Dose died before it was over, each of the two boys was to inherit a valley, and then each would have a property of like value.

Double-Dose's scheme became a real obsession with him. He went so far as to fix up the cabin in the valley he bought to make it nearly the same as the one he had built in the valley he staked himself, and he accumulated separate but equal sets of mining equipment for each valley. At the end of each mining season, he closed up that valley's cabin and moved to the other, remaining there for one year, and then moving back again at the end of the next season. Even though he was going overboard on this thing, it worked out pretty well. If Double-Dose had an equipment breakdown while mining in one valley, he could go over to the other to rob a spare part or a replacement for the broken machine, always making sure that the part or the replacement was later returned. However, he was finding it expensive to maintain two sluice boxes, two cats and two sets of peripheral equipment and tools. Since so much of his money went into equipment, Double-Dose was not getting rich.

In the meantime, Donald and Douglas were growing up. Soon as their second mother died, my wife took a special interest in those boys. We didn't have any kids of our own, so she sort of took them over every chance she got. Most every summer Sunday she insisted we take a picnic lunch up to Double-Dose's operation so the boys would be sure to get at least one good meal a week. She also decided that the twins had to learn to read and write, and Double-Dose agreed. So on most of the warmer winter days, Donald and Douglas walked the three miles down to the camp where my wife gave them lessons.

They were pretty good boys, though full of devilment, of course, like most boys. But to Double-Dose, they were a pair of priceless matched nuggets; I noticed that whenever I was around the three of them. Double-Dose just glowed when he watched the twins play beside whichever stream he was mining that summer. They threw rocks, poked around at fish with sticks, and spent endless hours building little rock dams to divert the flow. Double-Dose even set up a little toy sluice box for them and taught them to use it. To keep up their interest in mining, he'd go down when the boys weren't looking and salt that toy box with two little nuggets just alike. Double-Dose had in mind that they would follow in his footsteps, that's for certain.

Whenever most people in the camp saw the boys, they couldn't tell them apart. Double-Dose liked it that way; from the time they were little, he'd always make sure the boys dressed the same. When it came to those boys, it seemed to me that Double-Dose was like a dotty old lady with a pair of pet poodles who trims their fur just exactly alike, dresses them up in silly little jackets and bows tied on their ears just so's she can parade them around on twin leashes expecting everyone to say, "Oh how darling. Itsy and Bitsy are *sooo* cute." That maybe works with dogs, and even young boys, but when it comes to boys starting to grow up, I'm not sure it's such a hot idea.

Ol' Double-Dose was so insistent that those boys be two peas in a pod that I think he was almost blind to their real differences. Those boys did look the same on the outside, but my wife and I could see a lot of differences on the inside.

I suppose one way to describe it is to say that Donald was more a thinker, and Douglas was more a doer. When my wife was giving them lessons, she noticed that Donald sometimes picked up on things a little faster than Douglas, although the difference was not big. Whatever difference there was, it was hard to notice because Douglas was so much more outgoing. If he knew something, he'd tell you about it, whereas Donald was more quiet.

The outstanding thing I noticed was that whenever those two boys did anything, Dougy always took the lead, and Donny always followed. I saw that early on from watching those boys play down by one of Double-Dose's streams. When they built their little dams to make the water run here and there, I noticed that Dougy was the one who decided where the dams would be and who did most of the building, while Donny carried the rocks. "Bring me that big one over there," Dougy would say, and Donny would carry the rock. It seemed that he did not mind always doing his brother's bidding, but once in a while, if you looked real close, you'd see little signs. Like one time I watched Donny struggle over with a big rock, and then drop it so that one end fell on Dougy's foot. Donny looked real innocent when Dougy started to cry, but I'd seen the look of the devil in his brother's eyes when he dropped that rock.

Mostly, though, Donny just went along like he didn't have any initiative of his own and was willing to do whatever Dougy wanted. My wife was concerned about it. "I just wish Donny was more forceful," she said to me one day. "He just lets Dougy lead him around; it's not natural. I worry about that boy." I told her not to concern herself about it, because I'd seen other indications like that time he dropped the rock on Dougy's foot, subtle little things that nobody else seemed to catch.

Even though he didn't want to admit to any differences between the two boys, Double-Dose would let slip in the way he talked to them that he knew Dougy was the leader, and Donny the follower. "Damn it, Douglas, you two boys stop that," Double-Dose would say when they needed admonishment, most usually in a gentle voice that showed he wasn't really mad. Hell, he never got mad at them, even when they did things that would have caused me to tan their hides. "God, ain't they both devils," Double-Dose would aside to me. "Two boys more just exactly alike you'd never hope to see." Then he'd laugh and slap his thigh.

I thought things would change as the boys got older, but I got to admit you couldn't see any obvious signs. Before long, they were big enough to help Double-Dose with his mining, and even then I never heard them argue or tilt with each other like practically all brothers do. Sometimes Doug would make a remark that probably would have riled me if I were Don, but he just seemed to pass it off like he hadn't heard or understood it. Seemed to me too that Doug was getting more pushy with Don as the boys got older, yet it didn't seem to cause any trouble. I sensed that Don was just naturally one of the kind that doesn't like a confrontation and would go out of his way to avoid one.

Except for those differences between them, those boys sure were a lot like Double-Dose, real soft-spoken and generally pretty pleasant to be around. I guess that's why I spent a lot of time up watching

them mine in summer, on days I could get away
from the store. I never wanted to mine myself, but I
always enjoyed watching others do it. Double-Dose
knew I especially liked to watch the clean-ups, so's
he'd always let me know when he was planning one,
and I'd try to be there. It was fun to see those boys
work, too. By the time they were fifteen they were
working like men, and Double-Dose had taught
them more about mining than most of the other
miners in the district would ever know.

By that time, my wife had talked Double-Dose
into sending the boys off to high school during the
winters. At first he wasn't much for doing it—mostly I
think because he was afraid the boys would get interested in something other than mining. Double-Dose
had his heart set on having those boys keep on in the
mining business just like he'd done all his life. My
wife could talk a fence post into becoming a palm
tree if she put her mind to it, so of course Double-
Dose eventually caved in, but with serious reservations.

So the boys went off to school, and I guess my
wife had done a good job teaching them because
they both did tolerably well. When they came back
after the first year, they were wearing matched sweat-
ers like students do, and both had a big letter on
them that comes from doing well in athletics. Don
did not have much to say, but Doug was all bubbly
telling Double-Dose and me about how the twins got
those letters. Seems they had gone out for football,
and even though they were first-year students Doug
became the team's quarterback and Don was good

at catching his passes. To hear Doug tell it, all he had to do was instruct Don where to run and then lob a pass out to him in the right place—easy as pie, he said.

"How about girls; you boys meet any nice ones?" I asked.

"Sure, lots of them," Doug said with a big smile, but I noticed a frown come across Don's face. Uh huh, things haven't changed much, I thought to myself. Looked to me that maybe the boys had not done equally well in that department, and I remembered from my own school days how much girls always seemed to like the quarterback the best, especially if he was a good talker like Doug.

"Yessir, my boys is doing well," Double-Dose said to me after they walked away. "Two boys more just exactly alike I never seen." I'd heard that before, but I didn't say anything to discourage Double-Dose from his view. You can't show anything to a man if he doesn't want to see it.

And so it went, year after year, until the twins turned 17. That summer when the boys returned, the sluicing did not go very well. This was an even-numbered year, so Double-Dose was working the easternmost valley. Each of the clean-ups yielded less gold than the one before, and when the season was over Double-Dose barely had enough money to pay the bills and send the boys to their last year of school.

The poor season did not discourage Double-Dose very much because, like all other miners, he was so dang optimistic. I thought that maybe the easternmost valley had petered out, and I think the boys thought that, too, but Double-Dose was convinced that they had just hit a short stretch of poor pay. "It'll get better again further up," he decreed, obviously confident that it was so. Double-Dose's only concern was that the paltry return might cause the boys to lose interest in mining. They were almost grown up now, and might be having thoughts of going out on their own to do something else. But as they went off to school that fall, both agreed to be back in the spring.

Double-Dose moved over to the westernmost valley and was all ready to commence work when the boys arrived. The very first clean-up looked good that spring. It and the next more than made up for the poor showing of the season before, over in the other valley.

Then, for no reason that was obvious, and right in the middle of the season, Double-Dose started feeling poorly and took to his bed. He steadily worsened until that last night when he knew he would not survive. But he had died with a smile, knowing that he had had a good life and had done well by his boys. With tears in their eyes, the boys and I built a coffin for Double-Dose, and we buried him on the ridge top in the space left between his two wives.

"Guess it's time to read the will, boys" I said, taking it out of my pocket.

"Each of my two boys gets one valley and all it contains," Double-Dose had dictated to me. "So's it's all fair and square, if I pass on during an even-numbered year, Douglas gets the eastern valley and Donald the western. If it happens on an odd year, it's to be the other way around."

"Well, let's see, this is an odd-numbered year. That means I get the eastern valley, don't I?" said Don, unsmilingly. We all were remembering how little gold had come out of that valley the year before.

"Yeah, Don, looks like you got the short end of the stick. So much for the old man's wanting to make it fair all the time."

The boys stood silently awhile, looking down at the three graves and the valleys to either side. I could see that Don's mind was a tangle of emotions seething about in a background sea of grief still lingering from Double-Dose's recent death. I suspected that he was agonizing over the consequences of the will, probably feeling a touch of self-pity and maybe some resentment. He clenched his fist and his face was dark as he glanced up at Doug, and I thought for a moment that he might be feeling so angry that he was about to strike out at his brother. I was feeling pretty uncomfortable myself about it all.

But then Doug spoke out again. His foot had been toying with a little piece of quartz lying atop their father's grave, and now he kicked it away, saying, "What the hell, we could just ignore the will and keep on mining like Dad's been doing. Split everything fifty-fifty—we could mine together in my valley and share whatever we get. Then it would come out more like Dad wanted."

Well I'll be damned, that's quite an offer, coming

from a young fellow, I thought to myself. It took a while for Don to catch on to what Doug had said. I saw the angry look slowly disappear from Don's face as the meaning of Doug's words sunk in. Don began to smile, but knowing him as well as I did, I could tell he was still feeling a bit uneasy about something.

Finally Don said, "Yeah, I guess we could do that. You sure you're willing to make everything fifty-fifty?"

"Of course. You and I can be partners, and we'll call this operation the Dobson Brothers Mining Company. What do you think of that?"

"OK, let's shake on it," Don replied, now smiling happily, and I saw from the tear rolling down his cheek that he was overcome with what had just transpired.

The boys were on their own now, but not quite. I figured they might need a little watching as they began their mining together, so I hired a new clerk at the store so I could spend time every day or so up at their operation. They'd seen me up at the mining so much when Double-Dose was around that the boys probably didn't think anything about it.

Things went pretty well with them in their new venture. They each worked hard and seemed to take special enjoyment in their new partnership, one that no longer involved working for their father. They continued to mine Doug's valley and they stayed in his cabin, sharing equally in the cooking and household chores.

But it wasn't all roses, and I guess maybe I was

partly responsible for that. Thing was, the new clerk I hired was a young girl, just one year younger than Doug and Don. Emmy Lou was a saucy little trick, too, and just as pretty as could be. Her folks lived out of town, so she was boarding at our house, and my wife had agreed to look after her.

Don found out about her first, one day when he came down to the store for some bolts. Soon as he saw her he went all to pieces and could hardly tell Emmy Lou what he wanted to buy. After a while he got hold of himself enough to speak to her more easily, and quite a conversation ensued. It was the first time I ever saw anybody spend almost an hour buying just four little bolts.

Doug came in next, and it was a repeat performance, except Doug was suave from the start. I tell you, Emmy Lou was agog from having two young men playing up to her, ones that looked just alike, and more handsome than anything she had seen yet. "They sure are cute," she giggled to my wife one day, "I don't know which one of them I like best." And of course Don and Doug started finding all sorts of things they needed to buy or reasons to visit our house in the evenings. The two boys never came at the same time, and I never did know how they arranged for that. Since she'd promised Emmy Lou's parents to take care of the girl, my wife made sure she was around when either Don or Doug showed up.

On the days I visited the mining operation I started seeing more signs of testiness on Don's part than I had ever seen before in all the days I'd known the twins. Doug, too, seemed to be changing some, getting more bossy with Don than he was before Emmy Lou arrived.

One little episode occurred while I was up to the mine watching Don operate the cat. He backed it around a bit too fast once and crushed a large bucket used during clean-up operations. "Damn it," Doug yelled out, "you just ruined my bucket. And if you don't drive slower you're going to break my cat, too."

"Your bucket...your cat?" Don retorted, "I thought we were sharing equally."

"Yeah, we are. You get half the gold and I get half, but it's my valley, and what's in it is mine. Dad's will said that."

Don walked away in a huff, headed downstream. A little later he returned, having walked the short distance over to the eastern valley to get a bucket identical to the flattened one. "Here," he said to Doug with a superior lilt, "is my goddamn bucket. It's now yours." I was surprised; that interchange was the most heated I'd ever heard between the two brothers.

Then a few days later while I was watching them sluice, Doug walked up to Don saying, "We're going to do a clean-up tomorrow."

Don was silent a few moments, then he said, "I was thinking we ought to push more dirt in the sluice first. We're partners, remember—don't you think we ought to talk over something like that?"

I guess it embarrassed them to have me overhear that, and they both looked a little sheepish. "Yeah, Don, you're right," Doug responded. "I just wasn't thinking, I guess. Be fun to see what we got so far, though, wouldn't it?"

"Sure, what difference does it make. Let's do it." The little squabble was over, and all was sweetness and light again, as far as I could see.

I came back for the clean-up, and was it ever fun. Even as the boys removed the riffles from the box they began picking up large nuggets, one more than two inches across. As Don and Doug began to wash the box down from the top, we saw an ever-widening golden streak hang back at the upper end of the fines and gravel. They picked out the nuggets they saw and carefully washed the box down to its lower end, finally flushing the last bit of sand and the gold into the bucket Don had carried over from the eastern valley. Then for more than an hour we all hunched over the tub used to catch any escaping fines while we panned out the bucket.

When we weighed it up down at their cabin, Doug said, "Holy cow! We got better than 50 ounces. That's the best clean-up ever."

"And it's almost all large gold, too. Bet we can sell most of it for a hundred dollars an ounce," Don said excitedly. "We got ourselves about $5000 worth! What do you think of that, guys? I sure wish Dad could be here to see this. Wonder how come all this stuff is so big. It's nearly all large gold like you find in the top of the sluice box. Why do you suppose that is?" It was nice to hear them talk like that, and I enjoyed being there to see it, even though none of the gold was mine.

But then Doug had to go and ruin it. "I dunno,"

he says to Don, "but who cares. By God, this is great. Too bad your valley does not look so good." Doug jumped up and walked to the cabin door, opening it to peer up *his* valley toward the diggings, now located directly downslope to the west from the large cross that stood above the graves on the ridge top. Don remained seated, fondling some of the larger nuggets. For a person who was almost rich, he seemed strangely thoughtful and quiet. I guessed that Doug's remark had really taken away the pleasure for him. I could see that he was thinking that things weren't really equal between them.

He was probably thinking just what I was as I sat there watching them count their riches. Don was not really an equal partner in this operation, for he was participating only because of Doug's willingness. To be truly equal, two partners have to be able to bring like assets to bear, and that had not happened here. It was just a different version of the way things had been all Don's life. Double-Dose had insisted on equality in and for his boys, never quite realizing that equality is not sameness. Doug and Don were not the same, yet Double-Dose had always refused to acknowledge the differences.

The situation now was even worse than before. Double-Dose's grand inheritance plan had failed. Here the boys were, working Doug's valley, and living in Doug's house, yet Don had one of his own just a quarter of a mile away across the base of the ridge. And over there was a complete set of mining machinery that he owned—setting of course on what was probably worthless ground. How come his valley had played out, and Doug's was getting better? Then I looked at the gold lying on the table and realized that life was being pretty good to both the boys after all.

I was just starting to wonder how the twins were going to handle having this much gold all of a sudden when I got a fair inkling from their continued discussion—not really theirs, mostly Doug's. "Let's get at the sluicing again tomorrow. Don, you put the riffles back in the box while I grease up the cat, then we'll go to it. I figure we'll push through for another week and then do another clean-up." Doug paused, looked thoughtful, and then continued on a new tack. "You know, Don, I been thinking. We are using my cat and my equipment for all this, and it's my valley we're working. Maybe it would be fairer if we split the gold sixty-forty. Remember, Dad wanted it to be fair between us. What do you think, Henry, wouldn't that be more fair?"

Oh, oh, I thought to myself, time to get out of here. "You boys best work that all out for yourselves," I said. "I better get back to town now."

As I eased toward the door, I saw Don's face begin to burn and I heard him reply, "But you said...." Then he moved across the room ahead of me. He paused at the door, his face now looking more sad than angry, as he continued, "Yeah, well, I guess you're right; that might be more fair." Then he was gone.

"See you boys later," I said to Doug, and left.

The trail went down alongside the stream, so there was no way I could avoid walking past Don as he stood there all hunched over looking down into the water. I had in mind not getting involved in what was going on between the boys, but Don waylaid me with the first serious personal conversation we'd ever had, probably the first one Don had ever engaged anyone in, I suspected.

"Damn it, Henry, I did it again," he said vehemently, "I gave in to him even though I don't think the sixty-forty split is fair. I always give in to him, and always have, even when I knew I was right. Doug has been running my life ever since we were little, and I always have let him do it. What the hell is wrong with me?" This last was in an anguished tone of voice that made me feel real sorry for Don.

"Well...now...," I mumbled, not sure just what to say to the boy, and I wasn't at all interested in taking sides with him against his brother.

Just then a nice grayling skittered out from under the overhanging mossy bank where Don was standing. The fish did a little half-circle, then raced up the stream to disappear in the riffle above. "See that fish there, Henry; that fish is free. He's free to do what he wants. I've got to be free, too." Don raised his head, stiffened his shoulders, and spoke out with more defiance than I had ever seen come out of that boy in all his life. "O.K., goddamnit, sixty-forty if that's what he wants. But it's going to be just for this clean-up and the next. I'm going back in there to Doug and tell him that then I quit. I'm going back over to my own cabin to stay until I can sell my equipment. Maybe I can sell the cabin, too. I've been reading some geology books lately, and now that I've got enough money I'm going to go off to school and learn to be a geologist. Doug can spend the rest of his life mining this goddamn stream if he wants to, but I'm not going to have any part of it."

I was fair amazed to hear this outburst, so I just said, "Sounds like a good plan, Don," and I headed on down toward town, thinking to myself that I'd been right all along—this boy was maybe going to do all right.

During the next week I got up to the Dobson mine a couple of times and was pleased to see how well the boys were getting along. Don obviously had had his little talk with Doug, and I could see that the effect had been good on both boys. Doug was not being near so bossy, and even when he was, Don just let it roll off his back. Yessir, I said to myself, everything is going to be O.K. with those boys.

Unfortunately, I had forgotten about Emmy Lou, but the boys sure hadn't. One or the other was hanging around our house most every evening. Emmy Lou was having a ball flirting with whichever one of them was there, leading them both on just as innocent as can be. She wasn't doing anything wrong that I could see, but I was wishing she wasn't so dang cute, because I could see trouble coming.

It came on the night both Doug and Don showed up at our house at the same time. Up until then, it had been one on one: one saucy little wench, and one love-struck young man. Now all of a sudden we had ourselves a triangle. Triangles work real well when it comes to building things like sawhorses and house roofs, but they sure can be disastrous when it

comes to putting young people together. Especially
when it's an isosceles triangle like was sitting there in
our living room.

You can guess how it turned out. Emmy Lou had
said she didn't know which of the twins she liked
best, and maybe she was being honest. I think she
did try to treat them the same that night, just like old
Double-Dose had when he was alive, but what could
a young girl do up against the outgoing charms of a
boy like Doug? The more he talked, the more
Emmy Lou batted her eyes and giggled, and the
more sullen Don became.

"Oh dear, that was terrible," my wife said after
the boys left and Emmy Lou went off to bed. "Poor
Donny; he looked just like a little beaten puppy."

Under the circumstances, I decided it wouldn't
hurt to spend most of the next day up at the mine
with the boys. Indeed, Don was looking awfully sub-
dued when I got there, listlessly kicking rocks down
through the sluice while Doug worked the cat up
above, pushing pay dirt into the box from quite a
ways up.

I was standing beside Don watching him putter
away when I noticed that Doug seemed to be having
some trouble, like he'd just hit a big rock or something. I climbed up to where he was working and saw
that he was running into a ledge of some sort. The
bedrock looked like it suddenly jumped up at the
top of Doug's cut. He backed the cat up onto the
ledge and took a few swipes to push moss off sideways. I could see then that the ledge came almost to
the top of the ground; it looked to be solid rock

down just below the moss roots, real smooth-looking rock too.

Doug drove the cat back down below, gathered up one load of pay from the bedrock below the ledge, and pushed it on down to the head of the box. He shut the cat down, and jumped off, just as I came walking down beside him. "Don," he said, "I think maybe we ought to quit sluicing and do the clean-up. The level of bedrock is changing up above, and it's getting time to move the box upstream a ways. Want to come up and take a look?"

"Naw, what the heck, let's do it. I think we might be wise to shut down anyway. Look at what I just saw come down sliding right over the top of the riffles." Don had looked pretty sad a few minutes before, but now he was grinning broadly as he reached down under the sluice and lifted up one of the biggest nuggets any of us had ever seen.

"Migawd, Don, that's huge. Jeez, it must be four inches across. How much do you suppose it weighs?" commented Doug.

"I dunno, more than 10 ounces anyway. For sure, it's too big to weigh on our scales."

I stayed for the clean-up, and it was really something, far better than the one before. We found several more unusually big nuggets, and the entire yield was composed of coarse gold. It was so much fun that I forgot what this clean-up meant for Don if he carried through on his idea of quitting the partnership—this was the day he'd said he would quit. After seeing all this gold, I was wondering if he would stick to his guns.

Poor Don never even got a chance to decide. Soon as we finished the clean-up, Doug took the decision away from him with the words, "Well, Don, this is it. We split the partnership, just like you wanted, right now. Let's divvy up the gold and be done with it."

I wasn't too happy with Doug, but it was none of my business. I liked both the boys, and I wanted things to work out the best for both of them. Right then, though, it seemed like Don was getting the short end of everything.

The next hour wasn't any better either. I watched as the boys went through the decision process. From the start, Doug obviously coveted the big nugget. Don caved in to him. Still, he showed a little spunk when he proposed that Doug take it, and then let Don have first pick of the other nuggets until his share balanced the weight of the big one on a special scale we rigged up. He suggested that since the big nugget had a special value by virtue of its size, an equal weight of lesser nuggets would amount to a sixty-forty share. Doug rebelled somewhat at that idea, and I could see that Don resented the rebellion. He argued with silence on that one, and finally Doug agreed to the proposal. It went much the same way with the rest of the division, Don sometimes winning, but it seemed to me only when Doug begrudgingly permitted. For sure, it was a sixty-forty split—with Doug getting his way sixty percent of the time.

When it was over, Don looked just as sad and cowed as he had the evening before when Doug took over Emmy Lou. I didn't like the way things was going at all, and I could sense that nothing on this God's earth was going to change it. I was glad Double-Dose was not still here to see what was happening to his two boys. Things sure were not equal now, and Doug was not helping to make things any better.

He surprised me though, after Don said, "I'm leaving now," and began packing up his gear. Doug watched him in silence, occasionally fondling the large nugget and several other of his larger pieces. Then, as Don began to scoop his share from the table, Doug said, "You know, Don, we could keep going like this—I mean you stay on for a forty percent share."

"No thanks," replied Don, "I've had enough." Then a sudden flush came to his face as he blurted out, "Thanks, Doug, I appreciate what you've done for me," and he walked through the door.

While I finished my cup of coffee, Doug filled a pan with warm water and began washing up. He chatted away happily, saying that he might just walk back to my house with me. I saw what he had in mind so I thought I ought to let drop to him that Emmy Lou was back to her parent's home for a few days. Doug changed his mind about the walk, so I headed off by myself.

When I got down near the base of the ridge where the trail forked to go off to Don's cabin I was surprised to see his pack sitting there alongside the track. I glanced around and, looking up the ridge, I saw Don moving slowly up it toward the grave site on the ridge top. He needs somebody to talk to real bad, I thinks to myself, debating if I should follow him up or just let him be by himself. What the heck; can't hurt anything, I figured, so I headed up toward him.

When I got there, Don was sitting down at the foot of his father's grave, head down between his knees and sobbing. He hadn't yet heard me so I stopped, thinking then that maybe I had made the wrong choice and that I ought to just leave him be. I was about to turn and go when I saw him stand up and start looking around, a thoughtful and amazingly contented look on his face. He soon saw me so I walked over, and he did not seem at all surprised that I was there.

"You know, Henry," he said calmly, "this is a beautiful place. I've lived here all my life and I've never realized it before. I've been sitting here feeling sorry for myself. Then I got to thinking that for the first time in my life I just stood up against Doug by splitting with him. It was a hard thing to do 'cause I gave up a lot of money doing it, too. Sitting here, I suddenly realized that now I feel real good about myself. Then I looked up, and it was like I was seeing everything around me in a new way. Everything I see right now looks beautiful, like it was put there just for me to look at and enjoy."

Don's eyes scanned out over the two valleys, and then he said, "Henry, see how the low north sun makes the shadows of the aspen trees so long and beautiful. They all point up-valley, and up there somewhere they converge to a point. That point must be where the mother lode is, the place where all the gold comes from," and he chuckled happily at the fanciful thought.

I was feeling real good listening to Don talk like that, and he continued on. "Look over there on that slope, Henry. See those trees behind that rock sticking out, the real mossy one. I've seen that rock and those trees a million times, and they were just a plain rock in front of a bunch of scraggly black spruce trees. But now it looks to me like an artist's painting. Isn't it nice?" I saw what Don was looking at, and I guess if you looked at that rock and those trees like he was doing, you could sort of see a picture there.

"See the coloration of that patch of willowy tundra over there around that aspen tree? That is fantastic! The tree's a beauty, too. See how symmetrical it is, and how its leaves flip up their pale undersides as the quiver in the breeze. I've never noticed things like that before, but now I see every little detail, and how it all fits together."

By that time I was thinking that Don was going overboard with this beauty stuff, and I was worrying that maybe he'd slipped a cog. I was about to say something when I noticed that he was looking intently down into Doug's valley at the head of the diggings, directly downslope from our position beside the graves. There we could see the last cut Doug had made earlier that morning, and I recognized the change in level of bedrock that Doug had described when he quit work.

"Henry, do you see what I see? Look how the vegetation changes right there where Doug hit that bench. Just above, the moss looks thin and dry, and no brush nor trees are growing. See how deep and lush the moss is below the bench, and how much brush and trees are there. Then look up above again and see how that barren, dry-looking moss extends up-valley as far as you can see. The thing is, Henry, the lower edge of that barren area is abrupt and straight; it's right where Doug's bench is. That sharp line is coming right up the ridge towards us, too. See what I mean?"

I saw what he meant, and I was ready for him to tell me how beautiful all that was. However, Don seemed to have suddenly forgotten about beautiful, and his face took on an expression of thoughtful wonder. He turned on his heel and looked down into his own valley. "Well, I'll be damned," he exclaimed. "That straight line just keeps on going right down into my valley, but see how the vegetation is reversed there—the lush moss is on the uphill side, and the barren stuff is downhill from it."

Now that he'd pointed it out, I could see it, too. That funny line went clear across Don's valley, and it was located just a hundred yards or so above where old Double-Dose had quit mining there the year before. "You now what, Henry? That thing is a fault. I've read about those in some of my books. Yeah, it's a fault, a little fault that's hinged on the ridge top, yes, has to be! Its uphill side has pushed up in Doug's valley, and it's down in my valley. It has to have something to do with the gold—I wonder why." He paused a moment, then that thoughtful expression returned. "I got an idea," he said. "You wait here; I'll be right back."

Don took off running down into Doug's valley. A couple of minutes later, I saw him kneeling down on the bench where Doug had scraped it off. He seemed to be running his hand over the rock surface. Then he went down off the bench and looked carefully at the bedrock just downhill.

I saw him walking back up the slope so I sat down to wait, wondering what the heck was on Don's mind. He'd been a sad-looking boy not many minutes before, and now all that seemed to be over. Don came up to the top of the ridge, panting, but grinning happily. He took another long hard look at where the fault went down across his valley and then turned to me.

"I got it all figured out, Henry," he said with a big grin. "That rock down there on the bench in Doug's cut is as smooth as a baby's butt, and it's sloped parallel to the surface. Below the bench, the rock is broken and jagged. Its edges stick up almost like the riffles in a sluice box. See what that means, Henry? The gold has been sliding right over that bench and getting caught in the rough rock below. Those last two clean-ups we did were rich because, years ago, all the gold slid down through Doug's valley atop the smooth rock. Then it all got caught up on the jagged bedrock just below the bench.

"Yeah, that's gotta be it." Then he laughed hard, and I recognized a vindictive tone in his voice as he said, "Doug's just done his last big clean-up; the next one's gonna be a loser for sure. His valley is worked out."

What with Don guiding me along, I'd seen enough to figure that he was probably right. He seemed happier about Doug's impending misfortune than a brother ought, but considering everything that had happened, I could understand why Don was enjoying the thought of Doug losing out on something.

I sensed from the way he was acting that Don had even more on his mind. "Henry," he said, "I want you to promise me something. Don't tell Doug what we just found out. Let the bastard find out for himself; it'll happen soon enough. But I've got another secret that I won't tell you about right now. You come up to where I'll be working in my valley in about a week and I think I will be able to show you something really interesting."

"Hell, Don, I know what your secret is. You forget that I know just as much and maybe more than you do about mining," I said. "You figure that the fault cutting across there has brought Doug to the end of his rich clean-ups and the start of yours. You're going to go up and start mining right where that break cuts across your ground. If the fault is upthrown on the downstream side like it appears to be, that explains why your dad wasn't getting much gold where he quit mining there. I know as well as you do that the ground just above the fault is likely to be as rich as all get out."

Don looked down sheepishly. "Yeah, you're right, Henry, that's just what I figure."

"Well, it sure is getting late, near midnight now. I got to be getting home. I've tried to stay out of your business as best I could, but I guess I'll remind you now that when your valley looked like it was played out, Doug asked you to come in with him. You might think about that." Then I left, leaving Don still standing beside old Double-Dose's grave and those of his two wives.

Well, Don did the right thing, and he told me about it later. The next morning he went over to Doug's cabin and informed him he was going to try mining in his own valley. Don offered to let Doug go in with him—for forty percent. Doug suggested that it was a dumb proposition, and that he would be a fool to give up on what he had in his own valley to work for forty percent of nothing. Don must be out of his mind, Doug said, but if he wanted to he could come back over to Doug's valley and work for him for forty percent. Don chortled, "When he said 'work for him,' I figured he'd always thought about it that way. I was glad I'd gotten out, just for that reason alone. Then I told him he could take his pick, that I just wanted to make the offer so's things would be fair and square between us like Dad always wanted."

Doug did his next clean-up, and it was just like Don predicted, a real loser. Then Doug figured out for himself about the bench and the fault that caused it, because he was just about as smart as Don was.

I kept my promise to say nothing to Doug about Don's discovery, but I kept a close eye on things, and I was up at Don's diggings the day after Doug had his bad clean-up. By then, Don had moved his sluice up to the fault line and had used his cat to cut away the moss and soil just above. In the process, he had found the up-thrown side of the fault, lying barely below the surface. From the gravels just up-hill, he had taken several sample pans. The pans were rich, and one even contained a nugget weighing over an ounce. Don and I knew now that he'd hit the pay, and it was likely to be a real heller, too.

"What brings you here?" Don said, grinning, as Doug walked up to where we were sitting by Don's cut. "Things going well for you?"

"Sure, great. Couldn't be better. You know, though, it's not much fun to mine by yourself. Thought maybe I'd throw in with you sixty-forty, like you suggested. I can always go back over and work my valley later."

I could tell that Don was savoring the moment, and I got a kick out of it myself.

"Sure, why not," Don said finally. "I'd be glad to have you. Tell you what, I'll even make it fairer yet. Instead of forty percent, you get forty-nine, essentially half, more fair and square like Dad wanted."

"Forty-nine percent; why not fifty? . . .Oh, I see. That makes you the boss, doesn't it? Oh well, what the heck. Guess I can bring over my mining equipment, too."

I had to smile when Don threw in the final kicker, his voice far firmer than his brother was used to hearing: "Well, there is one more condition, Doug. We're going to call this operation the Don Dobson Mining Company. Things have changed."

They sure had. Under Don's supervision, the

Don Dobson Mining Company quickly took out nearly a million dollars' worth of gold from the cut lying just above the reef. It came at almost no cost, too, for none of the pay was deeper than six feet. The brothers took out so many big nuggets that they were not even inclined to argue over which belonged to whom. Besides, Doug was finding it harder and harder each day to argue with the boss.

I think Doug sometimes found it irritating, but as time passed, he really seemed not to mind. I suspected that he had always felt that Double-Dose had placed a double burden on him, and that now the load had eased off.

Later on, when I was up that way, I would see the big cross up over the ridge top, and I'd think about old Double-Dose Dobson lying down below. He'd died with a smile on his face, and I figured by now it had widened into a broad grin.

Before we quit, I suppose I should tell you about Emmy Lou because you probably realize that she helped stiffen Don's spine some. And you'd know that no matter which brother she married it was bound to cause all sorts of conniptions. Well, Emmy Lou went off and married another man and had a passel of kids—but she never got fat. I swear, if I hadn't already had such a good wife, I might have married that girl myself.

✹　✹　✹

The Lady and
the Dredge

Martha and George Swensen had never in-
tended to become gold miners, although
they knew much about it because George
had worked most of his life as a machinist for the
mining company that operated the dredges in the
area. Slight of stature and far from talkative, George
had apprenticed into the mining company's shop
even before finishing high school, and as the years
went by, his careful, cautious outlook and growing
skill had made him the company's lead man in the
shops. He had never gained enough self-confidence
in dealing with others to become the shop foreman,
but he was a highly respected employee.

George had rocked up onto the balls of his feet
the first time he spotted Martha in the hardware sec-
tion of the Alaska Mercantile Company store. Even
then, he was no taller than the pert-faced, rather
stocky girl who smiled back at him across the
counter. A month later, after returning to the store
numerous times to purchase sometimes only a single

nut or washer, George asked Martha out. "Of course," she responded with a hearty laugh, "I was wondering when you would ask."

Bubbly, vivacious Martha became George's wife a year later, and they settled into the comfortable little house located midway between the company shop and the store. They remained childless through the years, and Martha continued to work in the store. She convinced George to join the Elks, mainly because of the dances held each winter Saturday night. He went out on the floor reluctantly the first time, but before long Martha had him twirling her through polkas and schottisches with abandon. The Elk dances and other social occasions kept them busy in winter, and in summer Martha spent much of her free time out in the yard, growing the profusion of flowers and bushes that made their little home one of the town's showplaces. Each summer, she and George also frequented the creeks north of town where they fished, picked berries for Martha to preserve, and sometimes just drove around to examine the progress of the mining company's dredges.

On one of these trips they had driven into the valley where old Bill McKensie lived and ran his little sluicing operation each summer. Bill welcomed them and invited them to visit again. Bill was enjoyable company, and his place was so beautiful that Bill's valley became Martha's favorite destination for summer drives.

Martha and George lived simply, and over the years they accumulated substantial savings. The time came when both were beginning to think about retirement. They were idly discussing the matter over coffee one sunshiny Sunday morning when they saw Bill McKensie drive up and park outside their door. He usually stopped by to visit when he came in to town on a weekend, so the Swensens were not surprised. On this Sunday, however, Bill had come for more than his usual visit.

"I been thinking about selling out and going back to the old country," he said. "It's forty years since I've seen my family there, and now that I'm pushing eighty, I figure it's about time. George, you and Martha be at all interested in having my place? I know you like it out there, so there's nobody I'd rather see have it. Besides, if I decided to come back, I know you'd let me visit. The price would be right, and the ground pays well enough that you wouldn't have to work very hard to make an easy living. You'd get four good claims, George." Bill McKensie winked at Martha, then with a chuckle added, "Damn fine cabin, too; I built it myself."

George was so cautious and set in his ways that he never would have decided without Martha's urging. "We've lived in town all our lives," she said, "and almost all our lives you've been a machinist and I've been a clerk. Wouldn't it be fun to try something new? I really like Bill's place out there, and it's not far from town either; takes less than an hour to get there. If we sell this house and use only a part of our savings we can easily do it." Her enthusiasm finally swept away most of George's reservations, so in early June they bought Bill out and quit their jobs.

A few days later, with the first load of their belongings in the back of the pickup, Martha and
George headed out the gravel road that led up over
the ridge to the north of town. As they crested the
ridge they could see out into the next valley. Its upper forested slopes led their eyes down to where, off
in the distance at the lower end of the valley, they
could just see the top of the company's large Number 5 dredge floating in its pond, and beyond it, the
massive curving tailing piles it left behind.

Martha and George drove on down the road in
that direction until, two miles short of the dredge,
they found the little side road leading off to the right
along the lower north slope of the smaller valley
where their new home lay. They bounced slowly
along through the trees for nearly a mile before one
last turn and an opening in the forest brought into
view the little knoll on which their new home sat.
They had driven along in silence, but now Martha
exclaimed, "Oh, George, I'm so happy we did this.
Just look at it; it's a beautiful place, and I want to live
here forever." George smiled back at her, noticing,
he thought, that she looked younger than she had in
years. Martha had put on weight—enough that she
was now more than twice as wide as George, who
had not gained an ounce in forty years—but she was
just as chipper and bubbly as ever.

George eased the pickup around the final bend
and into the parking area Bill McKensie had leveled
off. It made easy entry to the little root cellar-like garage that Bill had built into the knoll sticking out

from the valley wall. Beside the garage, a wide set of stairs led up to the top of the knoll. There, out on the brow of the knoll where it overlooked the valley, stood the comfortable log cabin Bill McKensie had built years ago. He had repeatedly coated the logs with linseed oil, and now they were mellowed an eye-pleasing golden brown. Above them, the gently sloping sod roof with its wide overhangs was equally attractive, especially now with its lush green covering of new spring grass. When he put on the roof, Bill McKensie had known it would have been easier just to quit with the underlying waterproof tin surface, but he liked the old-style cabins, so he had added the sod.

Everything Bill McKensie had done was like that. He had an eye for design, he was patient, and he had a self-taught ability to work with his hands that made all he touched come out well. Still, the cabin and Bill's handiwork on the knoll were but capstones for what was already a curious and wondrous work of nature. The knoll itself was an anomaly, for it had formed some thousands of years before when, perhaps during an earthquake, a sudden failure in the hillside above had occurred. Thousands of cubic yards of soil and loose rock fell from the slope, leaving there a bowl-shaped cavity. The falling, sliding material had oozed out southward over the lower slope, and when it came to rest it formed the knoll. It stood against the slope like a buttress, little more than fifty feet wide, about as high, and just over a hundred feet long.

Once it had occurred, the cause of the sudden slide was obvious: underground water had lubricated the slope and made it unstable. When freed by the slide, those waters began gushing out of a rocky fissure, and the new spring trickled down over angular rocks below onto the base of the young knoll. A shallow depression in the top of the knoll had soon filled to form what became, as the years went by, a lovely little pond, not much over thirty feet across.

As soon as he saw it, Bill McKensie had fallen in love with the knoll, its pond and spring, and the little concave dell in the hillside above. The combination had attracted him so much that he had bought the mining claims surrounding the knoll from the previous owner without paying much attention to how much gold they contained. But Bill was lucky. After he used a little hydraulic giant to open a cut near the downstream edge of the claims, he found that the underlying gravels yielded consistent pay.

All this now belonged to Martha and George. Panting from the exertion of climbing the stairs, Martha entered the cabin, then went directly over to the kitchen sink. She smiled happily as she reached up over the sink and turned on the tap that stuck out from the cabin wall. She had always admired the cleverness Bill McKensie had displayed when he inserted a pipe in the spring at the base of the knoll to carry its fresh water over to the cabin, and also to the garden area that he had established between the cabin and the pond. "George," she giggled, "I bet there is not another cabin in the country that's got running water as good as this, and for free, too." Taking a drink, Martha looked out the window to inspect the garden that Bill McKensie said he had planted for her. She was pleased to see that a few vegetables already were peeking through the well-tilled soil.

A sudden movement lifted Martha's eyes to the pretty little pond beyond. "George, look at this," she called out. George came over, and they stood silently watching a mallard drake wheel around his mate as she sat sedately in the middle of the water ignoring his attention. George slid open the window before them, and they listened to the gurgling of the spring waters cascading over the rocks and rippling into the pond. The sound enveloped them, for it echoed back from the amphitheater-like dell behind.

Martha and George happily settled into their new home, and as the summer wore on they found each day just as pleasant as the day before. They soon came to realize that the little dell up behind the pond focused sunshine as well as sound onto the knoll, making it a bit warmer than the surrounding area. Yet even on the hottest days, the knoll was never too warm, because gentle breezes almost always wafted up and down the valley. Aspen leaves quivered chaotically in response, their lighter undersides flickering up in that gentle way that always brings to the mind a feeling of peace and well-being.

The breezes also helped to keep away the dense clouds of mosquitoes that infested the mossy valley bottom down at the base of the knoll. The knoll was almost mosquito-free because many of those insects that did wander up onto the knoll soon fell prey to the swallows that swooped and darted overhead. From time to time they interrupted their flights to zoom back to their nests in the miniature cabins that Bill McKensie had mounted on tall poles around the rapidly growing garden. The swallows were most numerous, but a few Canada jays, robins and chickadees seemed always to be about, drinking from or bathing in the pond. The two mallards also stayed, and they produced a brood that bobbed and skittered around the pond under Martha's watching eye whenever she worked in her kitchen.

Bill McKensie's cabin was small for the Swensens, so Martha talked George into bringing in two men from town to help build an addition during the early part of that first summer. Just enough room remained out on the brow of the knoll for it, and that fact provided a grand view from the big windows Martha insisted that George install on its east, south and west walls.

The view in each direction held its own charm. Martha and George could look out upstream to the east, where the little valley rose up toward a low dome, just a few miles distant. Up there, the north slopes of the valley were dark green where covered by stands of miniature black spruce and grayish green where only willowy bushes and moss grew. Aspen and birches shimmering on the south slopes made them appear as uniformly carpeted as fields of grain, bright green in summer and golden yellow in fall. Later, after the leaves were gone, the stark vertical tree trunks cast long shadows across the snow and no longer hid from view two little miner's cabins, long abandoned and with their mossy roofs fallen in.

The view to the south was much closer. By standing up next to the south window, Martha and George could see the stream that ran down through the valley past the base of the knoll. Between it and the gentle slope reaching up to the ridge top a half-mile away was the mining operation that Bill McKensie had developed. Bill's cut now extended up from the lower boundary of the claims almost to the base of the knoll. Out there was the large gasoline engine-driven pump he had used to create water pressure for blasting away the loess overburden. Farther down was Bill's sluice box, and downstream beyond it the tailings resulting from his mining.

Each time she looked out there, Martha inwardly nodded her approval as she noted how neat Bill had been in his mining. All the normal debris of a small mining operation—the numerous fuel and oil barrels, the pipe used to feed water to the hydraulic giant, and the odds and ends of cast-off mining equipment—was neatly stacked off to the side. Bill had even used his little cat to smooth the tailing piles, and most of them already supported a growth of fireweed and small willows.

"Now when you start mining, George, you do just like Bill; keep everything neat," Martha admonished as she stood looking out the new south window one day. "This place is too pretty to have junk lying around."

When Martha and George looked out to the

west, they saw a grand vista expanding out from the mouth of their valley to the wider valley beyond, a distance of more than twenty miles wherein no obvious sign of the works of man showed except for the cut in the trees indicating where the road from town and its adjacent power line came over the ridge and continued on out to Dredge Number 5, well out of sight around the hill to the right.

When the air was still, or the wind blowing gently from the north, Martha and George could sometimes hear the screeching of the dredge bucket line as it carved away at the gold-bearing gravels hour after hour, twenty-four hours each summer day. They found the sound rather pleasant. It reminded Martha that she and George were happily residing in a beautiful place, the effective owners of all they surveyed, yet not cut off from humanity. The intermittent noise was comforting for George, too, for it was the stable sound of the company at work—the company which so long had been part of his life, six days a week, fifty-one weeks a year.

Once he had the addition to the cabin finished, George began mining. He approached the task with trepidation, and spent the first two weeks fiddling with the equipment. He dawdled for the better part of a week over the little cat Bill had left behind, changing the oil in its engine and gearboxes, checking all its bolts and replacing a few of the parts, then checking things over again. But, much to his surprise, George discovered that when he finally turned the stream water into the box and began sluicing, he actually enjoyed operating equipment rather than just fixing it, as he had done most of his life. Once the mining work began, Martha came down to help, and it pleased George to have her there working beside him. She stood by the sluice with a long-handled shovel, using it to kick those larger rocks along that could not quite go through the box by themselves. It was an easy task, she soon learned, and only on rare occasion did George have to leave the cat to give her help.

They sluiced for two weeks. By keeping count of the number of times he pushed cat loads into the head of the box each day, George calculated that they had run just over 700 cubic yards of gravel and rock through the box during the fortnight. It was time to move the box a few yards upstream, so George prepared to clean up.

Even as he and Martha began pulling the first riffles from the head of the steel box they became excited. "Oh boy, there's another big one," Martha called out as she lifted the fourth sizable nugget out from where it was wedged into the riffle. Then their excitement increased as they washed the box down from its top and saw the thickening layer of gold creep along behind the sand and pebbles. That evening when they finished weighing it up and George did some calculating, he settled back in his chair and said, "Martha, Bill was right. It is good ground. That clean-up runs better than ten dollars a yard, and we never even got down to bedrock because the slope of the ground won't let me take out more than about ten feet of gravel. Do you realize that in two weeks we made almost half as much as I was making in a year back in the shop?"

Before they stopped work that fall, Martha and George did one more two-week mining stint, and that time they did even better than before. George then serviced all the equipment as Martha canned the last of the vegetables from their garden, and the two of them settled in for the winter.

They spent a joyous fall watching the colors change and the first snow fall. Large flakes wafted down slowly through still air and built up on the trees to give their surroundings a new beauty challenging even that of summer. Night after night the aurora came out to swirl overhead. Since it usually filled that part of the sky above the little dome at the head of the valley, Martha and George turned the lamps down and spent many pleasant hours watching the multicolored display out the east window.

Although for a few days in late December the sun failed to peek above the south horizon, they were not bothered, for the twilight hours were long, and even at night it never seemed too dark. That winter, Martha and George played endless games of cribbage and they read many books. They acknowledged to each other—George almost grudgingly—that this was the best winter of their lives, and Martha frequently brought up how pleased she was with their decision to move to the little knoll. "I thought the winter would get to me some, but it didn't," Martha said one spring day. "As I've said before, I'm happy to stay here the rest of my life. Maybe sometime I'd like to travel to the States for a few weeks just to see what it's like there now, but other than for that, I'm staying right here."

Seeing how content Martha was, George smiled at her silently. Always the pessimist, George suspected that all this could not last forever. He knew that someday something would happen to change it, but he said nothing, not wanting to cast any shadow over Martha's happiness.

The something happened even sooner than George had imagined it might. A minor alarm sounded the day he drove into town and saw two men operating one of the mining company's test drills near the mouth of the little valley. Nothing was wrong with that, of course, because George knew the company held all the ground upstream from Dredge Number 5 in the big valley, and also, as far as he knew, all the ground in the small valley up as far as the four claims he and Martha had purchased from Bill McKensie. George was slightly uneasy about the drilling, but he did not quite think through what it meant until later.

Then one day while George was greasing up his cat, he saw one of the company's pickups drive up the trail and stop beside the garage at the edge of the knoll. A tall young man wearing a tie and carrying a briefcase emerged and walked briskly over toward George.

"Hello, Mr. Swensen, how's it going today?" the man called out loudly and heartily as he approached George. Oh, oh, thought George, he's one of those religious fellows. George was much relieved when the man then said, "I'm Fred Sharkey with the company's property office. Like to speak to you a bit if I could."

"Sure," said George, shaking Sharkey's proffered hand, "Pleased to meet you. You must be new; haven't seen you around town before."

"Yes, I just got out of college and I've only been with the company less than a year. I understand that you worked for the company a long time. Heard you were the best machinist they ever had."

"Well, I don't know about that, but the company's a good outfit to work for," George replied, slightly embarrassed but also pleased by the remark, which he knew Martha had heard as she came walking up to them. "This is my wife Martha. Martha...Fred Sharkey. Works for the company."

"Just call me Fred, Mrs. Swensen. Say, sure is a pretty place you've got here," Sharkey said, bubbling with the self-confidence of the young. He gave Martha a hearty smile, which to her seemed rather false. Nevertheless, custom required that Martha invite the visitor in for coffee, and soon the three of them were seated at the kitchen table.

After some small talk while they sipped the hot coffee, Fred Sharkey got down to business. "I'm here with an offer for you. As you know, the company has been drilling the ground upstream from Dredge Number 5. The results are that the gold out in the main valley seems to be derived from this little valley. So as soon as the dredge has worked up far enough, we plan to turn it in here. The company holds all the ground down below you, and during the past year we have picked up the claims above you. We will of course need your claims too, so I have here an offer to buy, a most generous offer, I might add."

"No!" Martha instantly erupted, "We don't want to sell."

"I quite understand; this is rather sudden," Fred Sharkey said with a smile. "I'll just leave this warranty deed and contract we've written up here so you can look them over and think about it. Notice that in addition to a healthy cash payment, the company is willing to build you a new house in town or at such other location as is acceptable to both you and the company. Why don't I come back tomorrow so we can talk more about it."

"I don't think I like him," Martha said as she watched Fred Sharkey walk jauntily down to his pickup. He paused by its door, looking around as he lit a cigarette, then flicked away an empty packet out over the bed of the pickup onto the driveway. He revved up the engine, and soon was gone.

George was silent for a while. Then he said, "They are offering us a lot of money, Martha...and it is the company. They've been awfully good to me. And they do need our ground."

"Oh come on, George, you don't owe them anything," Martha responded. "We're staying right here, and you be sure and tell him that when he comes back tomorrow."

Fred Sharkey's hearty friendliness turned to polite firmness the next day when George reaffirmed his and Martha's rejection of the company's offer. "I hope you both understand that the company must have these claims," he said, with a hint of frost in his voice.

"Martha and I have talked about it," George said uneasily. "I sure hate to turn the company down, but Martha really likes it here. You can see that it is awfully nice here on this knoll. There's just no other place like it around. Now suppose we did let you have most of the claims—and I'm not sure Martha would go along even with that—but would it be possible to dredge around the knoll and let us keep this part? The place sure wouldn't be the same anymore, but it might be worth thinking about."

"No, Mr. Swensen, I'm afraid not. We've looked into the situation here carefully. We know how rich the ground is from some of the old miners' reports and we know how deep it is down to bedrock. You and Bill McKensie have been able to take just the top of the gravel layer. Dredge Number 5 is a 90-foot dredge, as you know, and even so it will just barely reach down to bedrock here in some places. Even if we left the knoll alone, by the time the dredge dug down alongside it, the whole thing would slide down and disappear. We'd have to keep the dredge out at least a hundred feet away, and if we did that we'd lose too much good pay. No, sorry, we cannot consider buying just a part of your claims. Remember, we now own all the claims both above and below you, so you can understand the company's position in this matter."

"I sure do," George said unhappily, "I been with the company a long time. But Martha....well, I guess the answer is still no."

"The offer stands, Mr. Swensen, and we'll keep it open for a while. Maybe you can talk some sense into your wife. However, considering your decision, I hope all the annual assessment work you and Bill McKensie have filed is proper and that your claim boundaries are exact. We'll look into it. You can expect to see our surveying team out here within a few weeks. Well, good day, Mr. Swensen. Let me know if you can get her to change her mind."

After Fred Sharkey was gone, George told Martha what he had said about the assessment work and the claim boundaries. Martha's face tightened. "The company would do that?" she asked, "Try to find some silly mistake that would allow them to contest our claims?"

"I dunno, Martha, but I think the assessment filings are O.K. I checked all the ones Bill gave us, and I've kept them up. They can't get us on that."

"What about the boundaries? Are you sure they are right?"

"Well, I suppose they've never really been surveyed, I mean with instruments. But as long as none of the claims are any bigger than they are supposed to be, everything will be fine."

"George, you go get your measuring tape. We're going to go out right now and find out," Martha said, but she unconsciously wrung her hands as she spoke. She then laid them on her lap and raised her head to look out over the pond. "They are not going to get it," she said, her voice firm.

Martha and George were greatly relieved after

several days of careful measurement verified that none of the claims exceeded legal size. "Is there anything else that might let them hurt us?" Martha asked.

"No, I don't think so, but I've worked for the company a long time, and I guess I haven't seen too many times when they didn't get their way. But don't worry about it, Martha, we've got them this time. Nothing's going to happen."

Nothing did happen that summer, except that the surveying crew showed up, worked a few days, and left. Fred Sharkey also came back a few times to renew his offer. Each time, Martha stared grimly at him as he spoke, and he never stayed any longer than it took to get the answer he did not want to hear.

"I'm really beginning to hate that man," Martha said one day after Sharkey left.

"On the other hand, Martha," George responded, "each time he comes, it tells us that the company can't figure any way to get our land without paying for it."

That thought was consoling, but life on the knoll was no longer as joyous as before Fred Sharkey's first arrival. Always in the background clung that gnawing fear that somehow the company would win. Not a day passed without Martha and George thinking about it, even though they spoke of the matter only rarely.

Summer wore into winter, and two more summers and winters passed before the day Dredge Number 5 poked its snout around the brow of the hill far enough to become visible from Martha and George's living room window. No longer was the screeching of the dredge's bucket chain an intermittent noise in the distance. Except when the dredge shut down for clean-ups or repair, the grinding of steel against steel and steel against rock, both day and night, was an ever-present reminder to Martha and George of how tentative was their hold over their domain.

Preceding the dredge up into Martha's and George's valley were the men who operated the company's hydraulic giants, the large water cannons that cut away the loess overburden and washed it down through the larger valley beyond. These men radically altered the view out Martha's and George's west windows. The gentle tree-covered slopes of the lower valley melted away over the course of two summers to leave a raw flat-bottomed gash nearly a quarter of a mile wide. It extended from the mouth of the valley where the dredge now sat right up to the boundary of the Swensens' claims.

Late in the summer during which the dredge first came into view, it turned to point menacingly up-valley toward the pretty little knoll, and as darkness began to fill the nights, the dredge master turned on the floodlights mounted on the steel superstructure and on little sleds out to the side of the dredge pond. From Martha's and George's windows the dredge at night took on the appearance of an awkwardly square battleship floating not far away.

Each day, Martha and George could not help but look out often toward the dredge. From one hour to the next, or even from day to day, the steel behemoth seemed almost immobile, but it was not. Like a giant steel earthworm, the floating dredge wriggled slowly forward to chew away at the valley bottom. While continuously extracting gold from the gravels within its long intestine, the monster spewed out the rock remains through the long stacker angling up behind. It generated the large arcing piles of tailings that extended from the bottom of the pond, 90 feet deep, to 30 feet above. From the little cabin on the knoll, the tailing piles looked like a close-spaced line of sand dunes slowly creeping along in the dredge's wake to engulf everything standing before.

Perhaps more than Martha, George unconsciously agonized over the dredge's relentless progress across the landscape toward them. His many years as a company machinist still focused George's thoughts on the dredge's massive internal machinery and its operation.

In his mind's eye, George could see himself high up in the dredge's command post, standing beside the dredge master as he orchestrated the array of chest-high handles protruding from the steel floor. These controlled the huge machine's slow but relentless motion. Mainly, it was a pivoting back and forth on the spud, a massive steel spike at the stern of the vessel that the dredge master ratcheted down into the pond bottom with gears driven by one of the dredge's many electric motors. And George was there with the dredge master as he controlled the sweeping side-to-side motion by pulling on handles that caused deck-mounted cable-hoists to wind up or unwind. Their long cables reached out to pull against temporary dead-man anchors buried just beyond the periphery of the pond. From time to time, the dredge master freed the dredge from its swivel point by actuating the spud-lifting mechanism. Subsequently, cables reaching out beside the chain of buckets to the forward shore beyond drew taut as, under George's approving mental eye, the master winched the dredge forward a few feet and then reset the spud. The slow sideways pivoting on the spud again commenced, forcing the bucket line into new gravel and rock.

But the bucket line was gnawing away at George as well, creating within him an internal conflict he could neither recognize nor understand. The habits of a lifetime dedicated to keeping the company's dredges operational did not break away easily for him. One side of George's brain willed the bucket line forward, while its other rebelled against the consequences to his and Martha's future there on the knoll.

Fred Sharkey drove up one more time that summer. George went out to speak to him alone because Martha was not feeling well and was taking a nap. She had been feeling poorly a lot lately, George thought, and he found that most disturbing.

Fred Sharkey was abrupt. "Mr. Swensen," he said, "the time has come to get serious about this. As you can see, Dredge Number 5 will be up against your property line before another summer is over. We need to get busy right away with the preliminary overburden removal on your claims. Either you get your wife to agree to sell out to the company right now or we are going to overstake your ground and take it into court."

"What? You can't do that," George replied. "Our claims are valid; you know that. The company's got no basis."

"You may think that, Mr. Swensen, and I might even think that, but we've got some pretty good lawyers, and a judge might not see it the same way by the time they are finished."

"You son of a bitch, get off my property right now!" George demanded, stiffening his body to bring his thin shoulders up almost to the middle of Fred Starkey's chest. Never before in his life had he spoken like that to anyone, and he was almost ashamed.

"O.K. Mr. Swensen, if that's the way you feel. See you in court unless you change her mind," Fred Sharkey said haughtily and drove away. Later that afternoon, other men arrived, and they began placing claim location stakes beside each of Martha's and George's.

"What are they doing out there, George?" Martha asked, anxiety shaking her voice.

"Just trying to scare us," George soothed, "Don't you give it a second thought."

However, George was very worried. He was worried about the company, and he was worried about Martha. He insisted that she go to a doctor, and after he had driven her to the clinic in town, he went over to see the lawyer who had always handled their affairs, taking along all the documents he had on the mining claims.

"It's my breast, they want to do a biopsy," Martha said uneasily, when George returned to pick her up.

The next few weeks were worrisome, mainly because Martha learned that she would have to undergo the major operation they feared. The only good news was that George's lawyer assured him that the company could not possibly win a court case. "Hell, George," he said, "It's total nonsense. I've seen the company pull that stuff on a few other miners, and the only one who didn't cave in was old Oscar Radavich, and they didn't do a thing about it. The company never did take it to court like they promised. They just waited 'til he died, and then bought his claims from his executor for a song."

Despite the lawyer's advice, George became increasingly convinced that they should sell out, so he again proposed it to Martha.

"No, George, we have been fighting them a long time, and I just can't bear to see them destroy the knoll and the little pond. We've got to save that, George, no matter what happens. And even if something happens to me—if they don't get it all with this operation—will you promise me not to let them have the knoll?" George knew that had to be the end of the matter for now, so he nodded his head.

That fall, just as freeze-up came and caused Dredge Number 5 to shut down, Martha had her operation. It appeared to be successful, but Martha was much weakened by the long siege of medication and therapy that followed. By Christmas she had begun to recover, and it helped that several old friends

from town came out to spend Christmas Day with Martha and George. But it was a happy-sad occasion for all present, because each had the unspoken fear that this might be Martha's last Christmas.

Martha continued to improve slightly as spring wore on, but then as Dredge Number 5 started up again and continued to inch noisily toward the knoll, she seemed to lose her zest for life. The dredge was now so close that as Martha looked out the west window she had to peer slightly upward to view the top of its blocky superstructure. She was especially distressed on the day the mallard pair returned, skittered uneasily around the little pond and then flew away just as the bucket line on the dredge bit into bedrock with a loud metallic scream. The ducks did not return.

Daily, Martha and George kept a close watch on the dredge's operation because they recognized that if the dredging was to continue, the next set of the cable-anchoring deadmen would have to be on their own property. Martha struggled out each morning to stand on the claim boundary in front of the dredge. She put her hands on her ample hips and for a few minutes stood staring up defiantly toward the dredge master's control room.

Fred Sharkey came one last time. "O.K., Mr. and Mrs. Swensen, you've been very clever in pushing us to the final offer. We double it to two hundred thousand, plus the house, wherever you want it built. We need your signatures now."

Oh hell, let's do it, Martha, George thought, and as he looked over toward Martha, he saw her staring at Fred Sharkey with fierce determination in her eyes. Then her hand came up to touch her dress front, just where her breast had been, and Martha's shoulders sagged. She turned her gaze over toward George's face, and he saw her look of determination fade into one of deep sadness.

Fred Sharkey's head bowed down to look at the floor, and he shuffled his foot uneasily.

"No, by God!" George suddenly burst out. Martha's shoulders came up, and she smiled.

Fred Sharkey stared briefly at them, and the look on his face could have been one of relief. "I guess that's it," he said softly, then spun on his heels and went out the door.

Martha and George watched through the window as Fred Sharkey descended the steps, but then walked past his pickup over toward the dredge. Sharkey peered up at the dredge master's control room, then raised his hands and waved them past each other three times. Unsmilingly, he turned on his heels, walked to the pickup and drove away.

Suddenly the bucket line stopped, and a profound silence came to the valley as the last of the dredge's electric motors spun down. The dredge master walked out across the gangplank to the shore of the pond, and then headed over toward the knoll. George went out to meet him. As the two came together, the dredge master, a man George had known for many years, said, "By golly, George, you and your wife have shut us down. Can't say as it bothers me any 'cause I'll go over and work Dredge Number 9, but the bosses sure are not happy."

"What's the company going to do now, Ed?" George asked.

"Not much, I guess. Can't do anything but let this dredge sit here until they get your land. The company can afford to wait a few years if that's what it takes. They'll keep it oiled up and ready to roll when the time comes. Gotta hand it to you, though; you and Martha got guts to turn the company down like that. I admire you, and I ain't going to enjoy it much when the day comes to put the giants to your little hill here. Sure is a pretty place. Be seeing you, George. Good luck."

Now that quiet and solitude once again descended on the little valley—for the first time in summer since Dredge Number 5 had first peeked its bucket line around the brow of the hill below—Martha began a miraculous recovery. Within a month she looked like her old self, and she and George again began to experience that feeling of well being that began the day when they first came to the knoll. The feeling remained with them through the winter, and the continuing silence of the dredge during the following spring re-emphasized to Martha and George how much they enjoyed life on the knoll.

With Dredge Number 5 now quiet, Martha and George could again hear the gentle rustling of the birches and aspens in the dell as the mild summer breezes wafted up and down their valley, and the loudest sound they heard, except for George's mining, was the gurgling of spring waters falling into the pond. The mallards returned that spring. This time they stayed to raise a brood in the pond, as the swallows wheeled relentlessly overhead throughout the summer. Winter, as always before, was also silent, dominated by the cloak of fleecy snow that covered everything and changed its color in response to the lighting of the sky. Martha and George enjoyed watching its brilliant whiteness in full sunshine soften to a pinkish hue during twilight, then shade over into the cold blue of night, tinged at times with green and red when the aurora swept across the sky.

And so Martha and George lived contented on the little knoll for many years, nine of them, beside the slowly rusting hulk of Dredge Number 5. Then even it disappeared, as did the other dredges in the area because the company by then had mined out most of the creeks and was closing down. On the day the salvaging crew came in with cutting torches and attacked the dredge, George said, "Well, Martha, we finally won. We'll never see that guy Fred Sharkey again."

"Thank God for that," Martha said, "I never did like him."

But one day a shiny green sedan with the emblem of the state department of transportation drove up and a man with a briefcase got out. "Well, Mr. and Mrs. Swensen, we meet again," Fred Sharkey said with a big smile. "Things have changed since I saw you last. My hair is getting gray, and I see yours is pure white. And now, I'm the right-of-way acquisition agent for the state. We're getting ready to build the new highway through here. It will run along the slope just above. I have a proposition for you this time that I know you will not refuse. You understand of course that my offer is backed by the state's ability to exercise the right of eminent domain."

Fred Sharkey paused for effect, smiling wickedly at Martha, and she stared back angrily in his direction. "Now don't get upset, ma'am, listen to what I have to say." His voice softened as Fred Sharkey continued, "You know, all the years I've come here to battle with you over this place have made me appreciate you and this little knoll. You are one tough lady, and this is a beautiful place. Now please listen to my idea."

Martha and George are gone now, but at Fred Sharkey's suggestion, the new highway has a turnout marked by a large wooden sign that reads "Martha Swensen State Wayside." Those who pull into the turnout can walk down a short flight of stairs into the dell. Most people pause here to look at the pond below, for often a pair of mallards is swimming about, and they do not seem to mind visitors. If a person walks slowly and makes no quick motions of his hands, the mallards just scoot off to the far side of the pond, and it is possible to go on out to the end of the knoll while they continue to swim about.

Two benches placed on the brow of the knoll give invitation to stop a while to enjoy the scenery and the breezes. A plaque here also marks the former location of the cabin Bill McKensie built, and which George and Martha occupied for nearly twenty years after they brought the company and Dredge Number 5 to a screeching halt.

Old Fred Sharkey is a frequent summer visitor to the knoll. Sometimes he just sits out there and thinks, but when they need it, Sharkey straightens the poles that hold up the little cabins where the swallows live. And each time before he leaves he picks up any trash that the young people might have left lying about.

☀ ☀ ☀

The Author...

Long-time Alaskan Neil Davis is known for his scientific career as a geophysicist and for his nonfiction writings—not just the eighty-some technical papers he has written or coauthored but also more popularly accessible books on matters scientific *(Alaska Science Nuggets, Energy/Alaska, The Aurora Watcher's Handbook)* and historical *(The College Hill Chronicles).* Less well known, at least until now, is his family-based interest in gold mining and appreciation for the role miners have played in Alaska—though his interest in tall tales has long been suspected by those who know him well. *Caught in the Sluice* is his first collection of fiction.

Davis and his wife, the potter Rosemarie Davis, built their own log home near Fairbanks. They raised three children who all still live in Alaska with their families—and who all took their turns as well helping to move ground at the family property in the Ester gold field.

The Illustrator...

Alice Cook and her husband John lived for thirty years in Juneau, in a house on Chicken Ridge that had been built around 1910 for the superintendent of the Alaska Gastineau Mining Company. Cook began her career as an illustrator with the Bureau of Indian Affairs, where she worked developing texts to be used in Bush schools. She later became an environmental education officer for the U.S. Forest Service. She is a member of the Sunshine Gallery artists' cooperative in Friday Harbor, Washington, where she and John now live—not far from the Davises' winter home.

Caught in the Sluice was designed and produced at the Ester Press, Ester, Alaska. Ester Press is owned by Lisa E. Sporleder, who operates the business out of her home, an old 1940s mining cabin situated about where Moose John used to live. (Lisa's outhouse is a slightly more recent structure.) The small cabin was moved to Ester some forty years ago from mining claims on Eva Creek, about two miles away as the dredge floats.

This text was set in Baskerville Old Face, with Clearface Bold display type and Showboat drop caps. The cover was designed by Paula Elmes of Imagecraft. Thomson-Shore, Inc., of Dexter, Michigan, printed the book on acid-free, recycled stock.